Gobbolino
THE WITCH'S CAT

Also by Ursula Moray Williams

Adventures of the Little Wooden Horse

Gobbolino
THE WITCH'S CAT

URSULA MORAY WILLIAMS

ILLUSTRATED BY

CATHERINE RAYNER

MACMILLAN CHILDREN'S BOOKS

Publisher's Note:
The publisher has used the first edition of *Gobbolino the Witch's Cat*,
published in Great Britain in 1942 by George G. Harrap & Co. Limited,
for this publication. It is reproduced here complete and unabridged.

First published 1942 by George G. Harrap & Co. Limited

This edition published 2012 by Macmillan Children's Books
a division of Macmillan Publishers Limited
20 New Wharf Road, London N1 9RR
Basingstoke and Oxford
Associated companies throughout the world
www.panmacmillan.com

ISBN 978-0-230-76165-0

Text copyright © Ursula Moray Williams 1942
Illustrations copyright © Catherine Rayner 2012
Foreword copyright © Joan Aiken Enterprises Ltd 2001
Author Note copyright © Kingfisher Publications PLC 2001

1 3 5 7 9 8 6 4 2

A CIP catalogue record for this book is available from the British Library.

Printed and bound by CPI Group (UK) Ltd, Croydon CR0 4YY

Contents

Foreword · vi

1 Gobbolino in Disgrace 1

2 Gobbolino is Left Alone 7

3 Gobbolino Finds a Home 11

4 Hobgoblin 21

5 The Orphanage 30

6 Gruel 42

7 The Lord Mayor's Coach 53

8 The Lady Mayoress Doesn't Like Cats 62

9 Gobbolino on Show 68

10 Gobbolino at Sea 86

11 The Little Princess 112

12 Punch and Judy 128

13 Gobbolino in the Tower 145

14 Gobbolino the Woodcutter 171

15 Gobbolino the Witch's Cat 198

16 Gobbolino the Kitchen Cat 228

About the Author 241

Foreword

When I was young, I had a lot of books about cats. I didn't see my father very often, as he and my mother were divorced, but every birthday he sent me a book, and at least six of them were cat stories – *Millions of Cats*, *The True Philosopher and His Cat*, *The Cat, the Dog and the Dormouse*, *Tinkle the Cat*, *Puss in Books*, *The Cat of Bubastes*. (I still have them all, which is lucky, as I'm afraid many of them are now out of print.) But one book I didn't have was *Gobbolino the Witch's Cat*, because it came out just after I had left school and was reading adult books. I had never read it until Kingfisher wrote and asked if I would like to write a foreword. Always happy to read a new cat story, I said I would love to, and read it in one joyful gulp.

Who could help loving Gobbolino? He is such

an endearing character that it seems impossible that he should have so many misfortunes, that he should not be able to find a friendly home in the very first chapter of his story. And yet, time after time, something awful happens and he loses his opportunity.

When I was young, and in the middle of a gripping book, I used to creep out of bed and lie on the floor, reading by the ray of light that shone into my room from the oil lamp on the landing (there was no electricity in our village at that time). I read until some adult came upstairs and caught me at it and gave me a tremendous scolding. *Gobbolino* would certainly have been read in that way, for who could bear to stop reading when the poor little fellow is trudging along lonely roads or through wild forests? Some of his adventures are quite hair-raising, especially the last one, when it seems impossible that he can escape being thrown down the Hurricane Mountains by the evil witch.

I wonder why the witches in folk tales nearly always have cats, not dogs or pigs, as their companions? Is it because cats used to be worshipped in ancient Egypt and other long-ago civilizations? Or because cats are so cool and self-reliant, giving us the notion that they can get along quite nicely without us, thank you – apart from a bowlful of food when they want it, a warm bed to sleep in when required, and a bit of stroking five or six times a day.

Surprisingly, although cats so often figure as witches' associates, there are not many folk tales in which cats are the heroes. There's Puss in Boots, of course, but he is rather a bossy, uncat-like cat. There is Dick Whittington's cat, another bossy character, persuading his master to turn back and become Lord Mayor of London. There's the cat who rushed up the chimney squawking, "My stars! Old Peter's dead and *I'm* the King of the Cats!" We don't hear any more than that about him. And I remember, from Andrew Lang's *Pink Fairy Book*, a touching story called "The Cat's Elopement". But apart from these I can think of few cats in folk tales – cats don't choose to have their stories told.

Poetry seems to suit them better. There are plenty of cats in poems. There is "I love Little Pussy, His coat is so warm," to which my father added the lines "And if I annoy him, He'll chew off my arm." There is a wonderful refrain in "Millions of Cats": "Cats here, cats there, Cats and kittens everywhere, Hundreds of cats, Thousands of cats, Millions and billions and trillions of cats." There is "Pussycat, pussycat, where have you been? I've been up to London to visit the Queen." And then there is Thomas Gray's cat who drowned in a tub of goldfishes. It must have been a very large bowl, or a very small and stupid cat!

Real cats, of course, vary in their natures just as

much as humans do. I have met spiteful cats, loving cats, clever cats, stupid cats. A highly intelligent orange cat, January, who adopted my father one New Year's Day, learned how to rattle the latch of the dining-room door, so that it would swing open and let him in. He also, all by himself, invented a charming trick: when you softly clapped your hands above his head, he would lift up his right front paw to be shaken. Then there was Gracchus, a tabby belonging to my sister, who used to come and stay at our house along with my two nieces for summer holidays. He was epileptic and had to be given a tiny pill every day. This aroused great feelings of jealousy in our cat Hamlet, who thought he was missing out on some treat – so terrific dexterity and diplomacy were needed to get the pill into the right cat. And then there was Darwin, dear Darwin, who always took a shortcut through the banisters, and liked to lie with his shaggy arms around one's neck . . .

If, out of a lifetime's acquaintance with cats, I were asked to pick one to take with me to a desert island, I would find it very, very hard to decide. But if I were asked to make a choice from all the cats in *books* that I have come across, the choice would be far easier. Not Puss in Boots – I want none of that phoney Marquis of Carabas routine on my island. Not Kipling's Cat that Walked by Himself – he would always be walking off. Not Whittington's cat, forever ordering me to turn back – because where would we turn back to? None of these would do. No – who but Gobbolino could be relied on to find a comfortable, snug home somewhere on that island, and lead me to it . . .

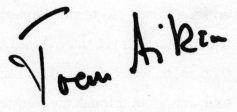

Sussex, 2001

GOBBOLINO IN DISGRACE

One fine moonlight night little Gobbolino,
the witch's kitten, and his sister Sootica
tumbled out of the cavern where they

had been born, to play at catch-a-mouse among the creeping shadows.

It was the first time they had left the cavern, and their round eyes were full of wonder and excitement at everything they saw.

Every leaf that blew, every dewdrop that glittered, every rustle in the forest around them set their furry black ears a-prick.

"Did you hear that, brother?"

"Did you see that, sister?"

"I saw it! *And that! And that! And that!*"

When they were tired of playing they sat side by side in the moonlight talking and quarrelling a little, as a witch's kittens will.

"What will you be when you grow up?" Gobbolino asked, as the moon began to sink behind the mountains and cocks crowed down the valley.

"Oh, I'll be a witch's cat like my ma," said Sootica. "I'll know all the Book of Magic off by heart and learn to ride a broomstick and turn mice into frogs and frogs into guinea pigs. I'll fly down the clouds on the night-wind with the bats and the barn owls, saying '*Meee-ee-ee-oww!*' so when people hear me coming they'll say: '*Hush! There goes Sootica, the witch's cat!*'"

Gobbolino was very silent when he heard his sister's fiery words.

"And what will you be, brother?" asked Sootica agreeably.

"I'll be a kitchen cat," said Gobbolino. "I'll sit by the fire with my paws tucked under my chest and sing like the kettle on the hob. When the children come in from school they'll pull my ears and tickle me under the chin and coax me round the kitchen with a cotton reel. I'll mind the house and keep down the mice and watch the baby, and when all the children are in bed I'll creep on my missus's lap while she darns the stockings and master nods in his chair. I'll stay with them for ever and ever, and they'll call me Gobbolino the kitchen cat."

"Don't you want to be bad?" Sootica asked him in great surprise.

"No," said Gobbolino, "I want to be good and have people love me. People don't love witches' cats. They are too disagreeable."

He licked his paw and began to wash his face, while his little sister scowled at him and was just about to trot in and find their mother, when a ray of moonlight falling across both the kittens set her fur standing on end with rage and fear.

"Brother! Brother! One of your paws is white!"

In the deeps of the witch's cavern no one had noticed that little Gobbolino had been born with a white front paw. Everyone knows this is quite wrong for witches' kittens, which are black all over from head to foot, but now the moonbeam lit up a pure white sock with five pink pads beneath it, while the kitten's coat, instead of being jet black like his sister's, had a faint sheen of tabby, and his lovely round eyes were blue! All witches' kittens are born with green eyes.

No wonder that little Sootica flew into the cavern with cries of distress to tell her mother all about it.

"Ma! Ma! Our Gobbolino has a white sock! He has blue eyes! His coat is tabby, not black, and he wants to be a kitchen cat!"

The kitten's cries brought her mother, Grimalkin, to the door of the cavern. Their mistress, the witch, was not far behind her, and in less time than it takes to tell they had knocked the unhappy Gobbolino head over heels, set him on his feet again, cuffed his ears, tweaked his tail, bounced him, bullied him, and so bewildered him that he could only stare stupidly at them, blinking his beautiful blue eyes as if he could not imagine what they were so angry about.

At last Grimalkin picked him up by the scruff of his neck and dropped him in the darkest, dampest corner of the cavern among the witch's tame toads.

Gobbolino was afraid of the toads and shivered and shook all night.

2
GOBBOLINO IS LEFT ALONE

In the morning Gobbolino heard the witch talking things over with his mother.

"I think we ought to apprentice the kittens

very quickly," she said. "There is Sootica, who is eager to learn, and will make a clever little cat, while the sooner the nonsense is knocked out of her brother's head the better."

So when the moon rose round and full the witch and her cat mounted their broomstick with the two young kittens in a bag slung behind them, and sailed away over the mountains to apprentice them to other witches, for that is the way to train a witch's cat.

They flew so fast, so fast, that little Gobbolino, peeping through a hole in the sack, saw the stars of the Milky Way flutter past him like a shower of diamonds – so fast that the bats they overtook seemed to lumber along like clumsy elephants.

It made him dizzy to look below him at the sleeping hills and rivers, the chasms and lakes, the watchful mountains and brooding cities. Little Sootica mewed for joy at their wild and giddy flight, but Gobbolino shivered at the bottom of the sack, while tears of terror dropped on his white front paw.

"Oh, please, stop! Oh, please, please, please!" he sobbed, but nobody paid any attention to him.

At last with a glorious swoop like the dive of a wild seabird, the witch and her broomstick came down on the Hurricane Mountains, where lived a hideous witch who agreed almost at once to take little Sootica into her cavern and train her as a witch's cat.

The kitten was so overjoyed she could hardly stop to say goodbye to her little brother, she was so eager to begin learning how to turn people into toads and frogs and other disagreeable objects.

Gobbolino cried a little at parting with his playmate, but the witch quite refused to take him with his sister.

"A witch's cat with a white paw! Ho! Ho! Ho!" she croaked. "You'll never get rid of that one!"

So Gobbolino rode away on the broomstick once more, behind his mother Grimalkin and her mistress, and although they visited fifty or more caverns before the dawn broke over the Hurricane Mountains, not a witch would look twice at the kitten with the white paw and beautiful blue eyes.

So they flew home again and flung Gobbolino into the cavern among the toads, and there he stayed day after day, till one fine morning he woke up and found himself all alone.

The witch had gone and Grimalkin too, the cauldron, the book of spells, the toads, the foxes, the magic herbs, the brews, the broomstick, everything that had once made magic.

They had all flown away and deserted him for ever.

3
GOBBOLINO FINDS A HOME

The witch and her cat Grimalkin had been so unkind to him that little Gobbolino was not sorry to be without them, but all the same it is a terrible thing for so young a kitten to be left all alone, and he spent some hours at the door of the cavern crying bitterly and wondering what was to become of him.

"Suppose they never come back!" sobbed Gobbolino. "Oh, what shall I do? What shall I do?"

But at last the idea came to him that if his mother Grimalkin and her mistress the witch had really left him for good there was no need for him to stay in the cavern and be a witch's cat any longer. He could go out into the world whenever he pleased and find a happy home to live in for ever and ever.

When this happy idea had struck little Gobbolino he stopped crying immediately and began to look round him.

The witch's cavern was on the edge of a

forest, but not very far away were fields and woods and a river, and beyond these must be houses and farms and cities such as he had seen from his ride on the witch's broomstick.

Surely somewhere there must be a comfortable hearth and kind people, willing to offer a happy home to a little cat?

Gobbolino washed his face and then his coat and paws very carefully before he left the cavern for ever.

He trotted through the fields feeling very bold and brave, till the forest was out of sight behind him, and there in front was the river, winding its way in and out of reeds and shallows, bubbling and churning like the spell-water in the witch's cauldron, or flowing smoothly, with bright fishes in it that caught little Gobbolino's hungry eye and made his mouth water.

He had had nothing to eat the whole day long and the sight of those bright fishes reminded him how hungry he was.

"Never mind," said Gobbolino. "Presently I shall come to a fine big farmhouse with a fine big kitchen, where they will invite me in and give me a saucer of milk and a corner by the fire. Then they will ask me to live with them for ever – Gobbolino the kitchen cat!"

As he said this he thought of his little sister Sootica apprenticed to the witch high up on the Hurricane Mountains, and he began to cry again, but after all, it was what she had wished for, so there was no more to be said about it.

Presently Gobbolino met a little bridge that

crossed the river from bank to bank. It was a very narrow bridge, no more than a plank, and so low over the water that the little cat could touch the ripples with his paw as they passed beneath it.

He thought he might catch a fish this way, so he settled himself in the middle of the plank and waited until one of the beautiful creatures should come swimming by.

Before long a lovely trout dressed in pink and gold and blue swam slowly down the stream towards him.

Little Gobbolino trembled with excitement and waited for it to pass beneath the plank.

He stretched out his paw at the same moment as the trout saw him and flashed by with a scornful swish of its tail. The little cat made one wild grab after it, reached too far, overbalanced, and tumbled head-over-heels into the water.

There was a terrible splash and commotion as he thought he was drowning, and then Gobbolino began to swim.

He swam and swam as the river carried him swiftly downstream, far from the forest and the cavern where he was born. He swam till the river ran into farmland, towards a great mill where the mill-wheel waited to churn Gobbolino into a thousand bits.

The little cat did not know his danger, and it was lucky for him that the children of the farm were playing on the river bank just above the mill-stream.

"Look! Look!" they cried to one another. "Here comes a kitten swimming for its life!"

"It will get caught in the mill-wheel!" said

one of the little girls. "Quick! Quick! And get it out!"

Her brothers ran to get a stick and fished out Gobbolino as they might have fished a plum out of one of their mother's pies.

"What a black coat he has!" they said.

"It is almost tabby!" said the little girls.

"And what bright eyes!" said their brothers.

"They are a beautiful blue!" said the little girls.

"He has three black paws!" said the boys.

"But one is pure white!" said the girls.

They took Gobbolino into the farm to show him to their mother.

The farm was fine and big, and it was the kind of kitchen Gobbolino had dreamed of.

There were red stone tiles and bright pots and pans sitting on shelves all the way round the room. There was a blazing fire in the hearth and a kettle singing on the hob. There was a baby in a cradle that rocked as the children's mother pushed it gently to and fro.

"Oh, what a lucky cat I am!" he said to himself, in spite of his weariness and cold. "Here is the first house I come to, the home of my dreams! A friendly roof, a good fire, a worthy mother, and kind-hearted children! Now I can settle down happily and be a plain little kitchen cat for ever and ever."

The farmer's wife took Gobbolino on her lap and wiped his wet fur with a warm cloth.

"And where do you come from, my little cat?" she asked him kindly. "How did you come to fall in the terrible mill-stream? Don't you know you might have been drowned?"

"Yes, ma'am!" replied Gobbolino gratefully.

"I fell in catching fishes. I come from the cavern in the forest up yonder, and the river brought me down here."

When his fur was dry the farmer's wife gave him a good drink of warm milk, and while she went out to milk the cows he amused the children and the baby by all kinds of strange tricks that every witch's kitten knows by heart. He made blue sparks come out of his whiskers and red ones out of his nose. He became invisible and then visible again, and hid himself in all kinds of strange places for them to find him again, in the cuckoo clock, in a teacup, in the farmer's shoe, till the children were tired of laughter and begged him to be quiet, and give them a little peace.

In the middle of all this the farmer himself came in to tea. He kissed the children all round, but when he saw Gobbolino at his tricks he suddenly became very grave, and soon shooed them all off to bed in a hurry, while the little cat curled himself up in a wooden box under the kitchen table that the farmer's wife herself had provided for him there.

"What a lucky cat I am," he said, as he tucked away his three black paws and the white one and closed his beautiful blue eyes. "Now my troubles are over for ever and ever. I am Gobbolino the kitchen cat."

4
HOBGOBLIN

As little Gobbolino slept sweetly beneath the kitchen table the voices of the farmer and his wife mingled with his dreams.

"Where did that kitten come from, mother?"

"The children found it swimming in the millrace, father."

"Kittens don't swim, mother."

"The children said it was swimming for its life."

"It seems strange to me, mother, that a kitten should find itself in the millrace unless somebody tried to drown it."

"It fell in catching fishes, it said. It came from the cavern on the hill."

"Ah!" said the farmer, and he was silent for a long while.

"Did you see the tricks it was after when I came in?" he asked presently.

"I heard the children laughing, from the cowshed," said the farmer's wife. "It was playing with a cotton reel."

"It was playing stranger tricks than that," said the farmer. "Sparks in its ears, sparks in its eyes, vanishing, popping out of cuckoo clocks – that's no way for a kitten to behave, mother."

"The sparks came out of the fire, and the children put it in the cuckoo clock," said the farmer's wife.

The farmer was silent again for several minutes.

"It's a strange-looking kitten, mother," he said at last.

"The children are very fond of it," replied the farmer's wife.

The farmer said no more about it, and soon enough they went to bed, while Gobbolino slept and purred and dreamed and the sparks died out of the fire, and a hobgoblin tapped at the windowpane.

Tap! Tap! Tap! Tap! Tap!

Now every kitchen cat knows that when a tap comes on the window after dark no notice should be taken of it at all. If it is a stranger looking for shelter, sooner or later he will wake the farmer up, but the kitchen cat goes on sleeping under the table. It has nothing to do with him.

But little Gobbolino, who had never been a kitchen cat before, sat up immediately with his ears a-prick and whispered:

"Who goes there?"

Tap! Tap! Tap! Tap! Tap!

The hobgoblin peeped in through the window and winked at Gobbolino.

He had a little brown face and a little brown cap, and he beckoned with a little brown finger, whispering:

"Come and let me in, my little cat, now do!"

Gobbolino sat and stared at him, saying nothing at all.

"What a lovely kitchen you have, my little friend!" sighed the hobgoblin. "What bright dishes! What glittering pans! What a pretty cradle! What a nice warm hearth! Won't you let me come in and warm my toes, my pretty one?"

Gobbolino only sat and stared at him, saying nothing at all.

The hobgoblin became very impatient, and rattled at the windowpane, saying:

"You kitchen cats are all alike! All selfish! All self-satisfied! Look at you warming your toes in safety and comfort, and look at me, all lonely and lost in the cold outside!"

When Gobbolino heard these words he did

not hesitate any longer. He remembered how a short while ago he too had been lonely and lost, and might be still if the children had not brought him into the farm. When the hobgoblin called him a kitchen cat he remembered how lucky he was, and trotted straight across to open the window.

"You may come in and warm your toes for a little while beside the fire," he said.

The hobgoblin slipped across the table and sat down on the hearth beside Gobbolino, leaving dirty wet footmarks all across the kitchen floor.

"How is all your family?" he asked in a friendly manner, giving Gobbolino's tail a friendly tweak.

"My mother Grimalkin has gone away with my mistress the witch!" replied Gobbolino.

"And my little sister Sootica is apprenticed to a hag in the Hurricane Mountains. I don't know how any of them are."

"Oho!" said the hobgoblin with a gleam of mischief. "So you are a witch's kitten?"

"Oh, no!" said Gobbolino shaking his head, "I am no longer any witch's cat. This afternoon I became a kitchen cat, and a kitchen cat I shall be for ever and ever."

"Ha! Ha! Ha!" laughed the hobgoblin, turning head over heels as if he thought Gobbolino was the greatest joke in the world. His somersault brought the farmer's wife's knitting off the chair, and in a moment it was tangled round the table legs, the pins were strewn over the floor, and the stitches running higgledy-piggledy after one another in greatest confusion.

"Take care! Take care!" cried Gobbolino, but the hobgoblin made one bound into the dairy and slammed the door.

Now every kitchen cat knows that no one may enter the dairy between sundown and sunrise, except the farmer's wife, but Gobbolino had no idea of it.

He trotted round and round the kitchen gathering up the wool and the knitting-pins, trying to set them straight again, but all in vain. When the hobgoblin bounced back from the dairy sucking his fingers, which were covered with cream, the tangle was as hopeless as ever, and there was nothing to do but put it back on the cradle just as it was.

"Well, I'm off!" said the hobgoblin, jumping out of the window in one leap. "Maybe I'll come back again and see you another night, maybe I won't. Goodnight, my little witch's kitten, and pleasant dreams to you!"

Gobbolino felt very relieved when the hobgoblin was gone, and he had bolted the window fast behind him.

"I have learned the first lesson of a kitchen cat," he said. "I shall never open the window again."

He trotted back to his box beneath the kitchen table and slept the rest of the night without waking.

Early in the morning when the farmer's wife came down the stairs she found her knitting in a tangle and all the cream stolen from the dairy.

Written across the stone floor in milky letters were the words:

"Gobbolino is a witch's cat!"

5
THE ORPHANAGE

The farmer's wife called her husband to come downstairs.

"The cream has gone!" she said. "My knitting

is in a tangle, and look what is written on the dairy floor!"

"I told you so!" replied the farmer. "Kitchen cats don't swim, and they don't have blue and crimson sparks coming out of their whiskers. Kitchen cats don't tangle knitting and steal the cream from the dairy. They don't put strange writings on the floor! He's a witch's cat, and no good to anybody. I'm going to drown him directly!"

But when Gobbolino heard his angry voice and saw him coming across the kitchen with long and angry strides, he was out of his box in one bound and out of the kitchen door, across the cobblestones, past the hayricks, and up the hill.

"Oh! Oh! Oh!" sobbed Gobbolino when he had left the farm far behind him and came to the other side of the hill. "What an unlucky little cat I am! Why was I ever born a witch's kitten? Why – oh, why?"

He was sobbing so bitterly that at first he did not hear the sounds of sorrow that came from a tumbledown cottage beside the highway, but presently the noise of sobs and tears and lamentations became so loud that his own tears ceased, and he stopped to look in through the open door and see what could be the cause of such misery.

The cottage was as wretched as any he had seen, while in the middle of it three little brothers were packing all their worldly goods into three red handkerchiefs, while a baby in a basket looked on and joined in their sorrow, which was very loud and miserable indeed.

When they caught sight of Gobbolino they

stopped crying immediately and rushed to pick him up.

The middle brother fell over the biggest brother, the smallest brother squeezed between their legs and brought them both down in a heap, while the baby tumbled out of its basket, and lay squalling in the middle of the floor, for he saw that he would never reach the kitten first, which made him very distressed indeed.

"Oh, you dear, sweet, pretty little cat!" cried all the little brothers together. "What is your name and where do you come from? And what are you doing wandering along the highway all alone?"

Gobbolino jumped lightly over their heads and tucked the baby back into his basket before he said sedately:

"My name is Gobbolino, and I come from the farm down yonder. I am looking for a home where I can catch the mice and mind the children and sit by the fire for ever and ever."

"Oh, do stay with us!" begged the little brothers, and then they suddenly burst out crying again and sobbed:

"Oh! Oh! But we haven't got a home any longer! We are orphans, and the house is tumbling to pieces! We've got to go out into the world and find a new house and a new father and mother! Oh! Oh! Oh!"

When Gobbolino found that the little brothers were in just such a plight as himself he took them all to his heart and tied up their little bootlaces and helped them pack their bundles one by one. Then he picked up the baby in the basket and led them out of the tumbledown cottage on to the king's highway, where their tears soon dried as they chased butterflies and picked great bunches of kingcups that they gave to Gobbolino to carry for them.

As they ran and skipped and hopped they talked about the happy home they meant to find, the kind father and mother, and the splendid house with large gardens and a beautiful nursery full of rocking-horses and a thousand different toys, with a golden cradle for the baby.

"And of course there will be a place by the fire for you, dear, kind, good little Gobbolino!" they cried. "You must stay with us for ever and ever!"

Gobbolino felt he would like nothing better than to stay with these happy-go-lucky children, but if he could first help them to find kind parents and a happy home he did not mind what became of himself.

They were so young and innocent, he felt it was his duty to find a father and mother for them as soon as possible.

They had walked for some miles, and all the little brothers were tired as well as hungry, when they came to some high iron gates set in a high stone wall. Written across the top of the gates in gilt letters was the word "ORPHANAGE".

When the little brothers read these words they clapped their hands with joy, while the baby in the basket crowed, and Gobbolino's heart fluttered with pleasure at meeting such good fortune so quickly.

"What a lucky cat I am!" he said, putting down the basket to ring the bell. "This is just the place I was looking for! Surely here they will feed these poor children and be kind to them, or who else will?"

Before long a kind, rosy-faced woman in a white cap opened the door, raising her hands in astonishment at the sight of the three little brothers and the baby in the basket, who all began talking to her at once.

"Oh, please, ma'am, we are four orphans and our house is tumbled down and we are looking for a kind home and a father and mother and a cradle for the baby and a place by the kitchen fire for Gobbolino our little cat!"

"My goodness gracious!" exclaimed the rosy-faced porteress, trying to fold them all into her arms at once. "Come in and warm yourselves and eat a bowl of hot soup. Who will be kind to four orphans if it isn't an orphanage? And who will turn out such a pretty little cat? Come in, come in, the sun is going down, and all children should be having their supper and going to bed."

The little brothers trotted into the orphanage behind her, while the porteress carried the baby in the basket and Gobbolino followed at their heels.

Soon the little boys were seated at trestle tables with four and twenty other orphans, and when Gobbolino saw how hopefully they gobbled up their soup, how often they passed their plates for more, and how cheerfully they banged the heads of the other orphans with their wooden spoons, he trotted into the kitchen behind the porteress in great contentment and thankfully lapped up the saucer of bread and milk that she offered him there.

"Such pretty boys!" said the porteress. "A father or mother would be proud to own them!"

And she told Gobbolino that in a few days' time the Lord Mayor and Mayoress were coming to the orphanage to choose an orphan to bring up as their own child. She felt quite sure that when they saw the little brothers and their pretty ways they would choose all three of them and the baby as well.

"And as for you, my pretty Gobbolino, we need a cat in the kitchen to keep down the mice," said the porteress. "You can stay here and help the cook and mind the orphans for as long as you please."

Gobbolino thanked her very gratefully, though he sighed a little at the thought of parting from the little brothers, of whom he had grown quite fond; but he liked to think of the kind home waiting for them, and of the father and mother who would care for them and bring them up as worthy citizens. It would suit him very well, he thought, to become an orphanage cat, and although the cook was very sour-faced and bad-tempered, the porteress was very kind.

So he slept well enough on the piece of old carpet that the cook threw at him, and was up early in the morning watching at the mouseholes in the hope of showing what he was worth by the time the cook came downstairs.

A witch's kitten is always an excellent mouser.

Gobbolino had only to turn himself into a piece of Stilton cheese and wait outside the mousehole.

Presently, *sniff-sniff-sniff! Scrabble-scrabble-scrabble!* The mouse came down the wainscot sniffing with its pointed nose and twitching its greedy whiskers. It crept into the kitchen and looked about for the cook, but there was nobody there – only a tempting piece of Stilton cheese lying on the shiny red tiles.

Sniff-sniff-sniff! The mouse crept closer and closer, and then all of a sudden Gobbolino was a cat again, and there was one thief the less in the kitchen – for the mice stole the orphans' cake and ran all over the larder leaving dirty little footmarks on all the food, doing nearly as much damage as the hobgoblin.

6
GRUEL

Gobbolino had caught three mice by the time
the cook came downstairs, but she would not
look at him or give him a word of praise.

She set about making gruel for the orphans' breakfast. It was very thin and grey and unpleasant, and the orphans hated it. The porteress had told the cook to make them good porridge, but she never woke up herself until the tables were cleared. So the lazy cook made gruel day after day, and the porteress knew nothing whatever about it.

When Gobbolino saw the unpleasant grey mixture that the cook was stirring in the cauldron he felt sorry for the orphans, and when her back was turned he put a spell into the gruel that filled it full of sugar-plums.

No wonder their eyes shone with pleasure as their little bowls were filled, no wonder that they scraped them clean and shining so that the cook could hardly believe her eyes when the cauldron came back empty into the kitchen. She was accustomed to giving most of the gruel to the pigs.

The next day Gobbolino put caramels into the gruel, and the orphans shouted for joy. He also caught five mice for the cook, but she never gave him a word of praise, although he made himself as useful as ten kitchen maids about the kitchen, wiping the dishes, peeling the potatoes, and polishing all the orphans' little boots.

The little brothers romped joyfully with the other orphans, playing at hide-and-seek, touch last, follow my leader, and other nursery games. The baby sat on the porteress's lap and sucked its thumb. It gladdened Gobbolino's heart to see them so contented and happy.

When he crept into the nursery to see how they were doing the little brothers flew to clasp him round the neck.

"Oh, our dear, our darling, our beautiful Gobbolino!" they shouted, while the baby crowed and kicked, but they had no time to make a fuss of him before the cook called him back to the kitchen. She said that the mice came out and jeered at her when he was out of the way.

The next day all was bustle and confusion, for the Lord Mayor and his lady were coming on the morrow to choose an orphan to bring up as their own child, and everything in the orphanage was made ready to receive them.

All the orphans' best white frocks and shirts must be starched and ironed, their hair put in curlers, their nails cut, and their shoes polished; in the evening Gobbolino helped the cook and the porteress to bath them, every one, with many shouts and splashings and a great deal of water over the kitchen floor, which annoyed the cook very much indeed.

The orphans that were being bathed by the cook tried to escape from her to Gobbolino:

"Oh dear, kind Gobbolino – do come and bath us! Oh, do!"

When the little brothers fell into the bony hands of the cook they cried and screamed and made such a fuss that she boxed their ears in desperation and left the kitchen, to the great joy of all the orphans, who skipped about the floor in their little nightshirts crying "Hurrah! Hurrah! Hurrah!" till even Gobbolino grew a little weary of them.

In the morning the cook was still so angry that she put salt into the gruel instead of sugar, and all the sugar-plums in the world could not hide the taste of it, so Gobbolino made another spell and turned it into chocolate sauce.

No wonder that the orphans' eyes grew round with wonder and delight as they sat round the table in their clean white frocks and shirts, covered with clean white bibs, all ready for the Lord Mayor's visit. No wonder that they polished all their little bowls until not a scrap was left, and then dug their wooden spoons into the cauldron and polished that too till it gleamed and shone, and Gobbolino, watching from the doorway, purred with joy to see them all so happy.

But when the cook came up from the kitchen to fetch away the cauldron her eyes nearly started out of her head, for the orphans' rosy cheeks were covered with chocolate sauce, and so were their clean white bibs, put on in the Lord Mayor's honour. No wonder that their faces shone with pleasure, or that their bowls were so clean and polished.

The cook rushed away to call the porteress, who appeared in her nightcap, blinking with sleep, for she was no early riser.

When she heard the cook's story and saw the orphans' bibs she turned quite pale.

"Where have you come from, my little cat?" she asked Gobbolino. "And who was your mother?"

"Please, ma'am, I was born in a witch's cave and Grimalkin was my mother!" replied Gobbolino innocently. "My little sister Sootica is apprenticed to a witch in the Hurricane Mountains, but I wished to become a kitchen cat, so I left home, and here I am!"

"I knew it! I was positive of it!" stormed the

cook. "Only a witch's cat could do such things! No cat could kill so many mice without the aid of magic. He may cast spells on the children! He may turn us all into herrings or bats or horrible reptiles! Do away with him directly, ma'am! Don't keep such a creature among innocent babies!"

The eyes of the honest porteress filled with tears as she looked at Gobbolino, for she had no heart to turn even a witch's kitten out of doors, while all the orphans set up such a weeping and a wailing (particularly the little brothers) that they threatened to ruin all their best starched shirts and dresses as well as their dirty bibs, stretching out their arms and sobbing:

"Oh, don't send away our dear, darling, beautiful Gobbolino!"

And in the middle of it all the Lord Mayor's coach rolled up to the door, and the Lord Mayor's coachman pulled the bell.

The porteress had just time to dry the orphans' tears, wipe the chocolate sauce off their faces and remove their bibs, while the cook, having flung her slipper at Gobbolino and driven him into the kitchen, ran to open the door.

The orphans were ready with bows and curtseys and shy smiles of excitement when the Lord Mayor and Mayoress came into the hall, but the cook bounced back into the kitchen and slammed the door behind her.

"Now be off with you!" she cried to Gobbolino. "Witch's cat! Magic maker! You shall never put spells into my cauldron again! Out into the street you go, and let me never see a whisker of your face again!"

So saying she picked up a stick and chased Gobbolino out of the back door into the street.

The little cat shivered and shook when he found himself safe round the corner.

"Oh, my goodness, how unlucky I am!" he said to himself, sitting down for a moment to get his breath. "I never meant any harm, I only meant to give some pleasure to those innocent children! Who would have thought it would lead to such trouble? Oh, why was I born a witch's cat – oh, why?"

But as he became calmer he began to think that after all it might be for the best. The little brothers and the baby, all of whom he loved dearly, were about to be adopted by the Lord Mayor and given a happy home. They would certainly be well brought up, and the baby would have a stately cradle.

As for himself, the cook had never liked him, and would sooner or later have turned him out.

He sighed to think of the orphans' gruel, but the porteress presided over the rest of their meals and they had nothing to complain of.

"Some day I shall find a happy home," said Gobbolino, trotting along in the dust, and purring to think of the good fortune that had come to the little brothers.

7
THE LORD MAYOR'S COACH

Gobbolino had not left the orphanage more than two miles behind him when he heard a far-off sound like the rolling of distant wheels and the galloping of horses.

With his ears a-prick he jumped lightly out of the road in case the coach should run him over in its haste, for on the road behind him a cloud of dust was coming nearer and nearer with such a thundering of hoofs, jingling of harness, and creaking of wheels as Gobbolino had never heard before.

Presently he could distinguish four grey horses driven at a furious speed, and could even hear the shouts of the driver urging them on faster and faster and faster.

"Oh, my goodness!" said Gobbolino. "That looks remarkably like the Lord Mayor's coach which I saw standing at the orphanage door! If it really is so, he must have left in a hurry! Whatever can be the matter?"

He crouched against the roadside while the

great coach thundered past, swaying and jolting like a clumsy elephant, but it had scarcely passed him before three voices called out:

"Oh! Oh! Oh! Our darling, beautiful, sweet Gobbolino! Stop the coach! Stop! Stop! Stop! He's here! He's here! He's here!"

And to Gobbolino's horror and surprise he saw that the galloping coach with the sweating frantic horses and flying wheels was driven by the biggest of the three little brothers.

Two more leaned out of the windows, calling his name with all their might, while the baby, slung on the axle in his basket, solemnly sucked his thumb amid all the jolting and swinging and said nothing at all.

When they saw Gobbolino, Big Brother made a tremendous effort to draw in his horses, but they were galloping so fast that he only bewildered them. The coach swerved wildly round the next corner, catching the wheel hub on a large stone, and overturned. The next minute with a terrible crackling of shafts and splintering of gilded wood they were all upside down in the ditch.

"Oh, my goodness!" cried Gobbolino, galloping after them.

The horses were unharmed, and although all the little brothers were crying bitterly with distress and bruises on their foreheads, they were not sorely hurt either. The baby had been tossed on to the grass and was already picking dandelions, but the Lord Mayor's beautiful golden coach lay in the ditch with broken shafts.

Gobbolino set the little brothers on their feet, prodding them for broken limbs in some anxiety. When he found they were all safe and sound, he cuffed their ears soundly all round, took the dandelions out of the baby's mouth and said:

"You ought to be ashamed of yourselves, you ought. I don't know what in the world is to become of you! The Lord Mayor will never adopt you now!"

"Oh, please, don't be angry with us, dear, sweet, kind Gobbolino!" sobbed the little brothers, bursting into fresh tears of grief and remorse. "How could you run away and leave us and not expect us to come after you and fetch you back again? How can you expect us to be adopted and leave you behind? We didn't mean any harm! How can you be so angry with us, Gobbolino?"

"Well, well, well, it can't be helped now,"

said Gobbolino, wiping away their tears. "I suppose the coach can be mended, and the horses seem as fresh as ever. We must go back to the orphanage and ask the Lord Mayor's pardon directly."

Big Brother caught the horses and mounted the leader. Brother climbed on the second and Little Brother on the third. Gobbolino leapt lightly on the fourth, holding the baby in his basket in front of him. The horses were no longer excited and unmanageable; they trotted quietly back to the orphanage gate and stopped in front of the door.

They found the whole orphanage, the Mayor and Mayoress, the porteress, the four and twenty orphans – even the cook, assembled on the steps peering anxiously down the road.

When they saw the little brothers the Lord

Mayor was the first to gather them into his arms.

"Oh, my poor, unfortunate children!" he cried. "You might have been killed or terribly injured! You might have broken your legs or cracked your skulls, or been thrown out into the road! When you become my sons you shall never, never run into such danger again!"

The Lady Mayoress hugged the baby in its basket and exclaimed in horror at the dandelion stains on its fingers.

"We must send for a new coach and take them home with us directly!" she said.

"They ought to be beaten!" said the cook disappearing into the kitchen, but the porteress had already found out about the gruel and dismissed her.

By the time the porteress had put arnica on

the bruises of the three little brothers and had scolded them well and told them to behave and kissed the baby and blown all their noses and kissed them again, the Lord Mayor's second-best coach was at the door and it was time for them to start for their new home.

The Lady Mayoress took the baby on her lap, the three little brothers scrambled aboard, quarrelling as to which should sit next to the driver, and the coachman was just cracking his whip when the boys cried out in chorus:

"Gobbolino! Gobbolino! Where is Gobbolino? – please, oh please, kind sir, don't take us away without our little cat!"

The kind-hearted Lord Mayor was ready to do anything for his four new sons, but the Lady Mayoress detested cats.

Gobbolino might have been left behind again

had not the baby stretched out its little arms so pleadingly that the Lady Mayoress herself opened the door, and Gobbolino jumped inside. He was careful to avoid distressing her by sitting very quietly in a far corner of the carriage, and so the coach rumbled steadily towards their new home, and Gobbolino realized with pleasure that he was now to become a Lord Mayor's cat.

8
THE LADY MAYORESS
DOESN'T LIKE CATS

The Lord Mayor's house was large and noble, and the nurseries more splendid even than the little brothers had dreamed of.

There was a golden cradle for the baby, a rocking-horse, soldiers, engines, and a thousand different toys in cupboards and on shelves around the room.

There was a thick warm rug in front of the fire where Gobbolino might tuck in his paws and drowsily watch their play, and a high windowsill where he could sit and look down upon the courtyard, with the Lord Mayor's lackeys running to and fro, the peacocks that sometimes strayed from the Lady Mayoress's garden, and the messengers that were constantly bringing great sealed letters to the door.

The Lord Mayor and his lady were as kind and as loving as any parents the little brothers could wish for, the nurseries rang with laughter and happiness; it was the house of Gobbolino's dreams – if only the Lady Mayoress had liked cats.

She tried to hide it, for she had a heart of gold and dearly loved the little brothers; but when she came into the nursery and saw Gobbolino there she turned pale and put her hand to her heart as though she might faint away. When she saw the baby cuddling him she shrieked aloud, and if any of the little brothers carried him near her she begged him with tears in her eyes not to let Gobbolino touch her on any account.

Gobbolino hated to displease her, and learned to hide whenever he heard her step on the stair, but she knew by a strange instinct when he was in the room, and as the little brothers would not let him leave without them, he spent many an hour crouching under the nursery table and wishing he had never been born a witch's cat.

"For if I were a common nursery tabby or tom, her ladyship would not feel so nervous about me," he told himself.

The Lady Mayoress became quite thin and ill, for all that the Mayor, the little brothers and even the baby could do to rouse her. The mere sight of Gobbolino set her shivering, till it was quite evident that she must soon take to her bed or pine away altogether.

But before this happened Gobbolino had made up his mind he would go.

He told the little brothers this, and their sobs, tears and lamentations filled the nursery, nearly breaking Gobbolino's heart.

"You love your kind new parents, the Lord Mayor and Mayoress, don't you?" said Gobbolino.

"Oh, yes!" said the little brothers.

"You are very grateful to them, aren't you?" said Gobbolino.

"Oh, yes! Yes!"

"You would do anything in the world to please them and bring them joy?"

"Oh, yes! Yes! Yes!"

"Then stay with them and be good, dutiful, loving children," said Gobbolino. "And don't mind about me. Some day I will come back again and see what fine big boys you have become. I'm off to find a kitchen fire where there is room and a saucer of milk for a little cat, and there I shall stay for ever and ever. Goodbye!"

"Goodbye, our kind, good, faithful Gobbolino!" sobbed the little brothers, so smothering him with their kisses and their embraces that he was not sorry to escape from their hands and scamper away down the back stairs.

The Lord Mayor with his pocket full of sugar-plums stopped the little boys' tears, and Gobbolino once again heard their joyful cries as he left the courtyard and trotted out into the wide world.

"Surely this time I shall be lucky!" said Gobbolino.

9
GOBBOLINO ON SHOW

By evening Gobbolino came to a town.

The lights in the windows winked at him like yellow and friendly eyes: "Come in! Come in!"

In a hundred happy homes the kettle was singing on the hob; fat, comfortable tabbies, careless of their good fortune, dozed under chairs, or grumbled at the noise the children made, bouncing in from school. Fires crackled frostily, and sleepy canaries, with dusters over their cages, twittered a last note before tucking their downy heads under their wings.

It was the teatime hour, the hour when every cat is lord of his house, and every house without a cat is lonely. Every cat without a house is lonelier still, and Gobbolino trotted along missing the bright nursery fire, missing the noisy clatter of the little brothers, missing the chuckle of the baby, the clamour of the orphanage, the comfort of the farm kitchen, missing even the gloomy cavern where he had been born. He belonged to nobody, and nobody belonged to him.

He jumped on to a windowsill, peeping in through the lace curtains.

The room that he peeped into was very strange.

There was an ordinary table in the middle, certainly, and some chairs, and a kettle on the hob that sang and hissed. There were saucepans and a teapot and a blue-and-white china tea set and a clock that had lost one hand, but all the way round the room were dozens of large cages, and in each cage, sitting on a blue velvet cushion, was a cat.

A little old man stood at the table cutting up cat's-meat on twelve blue china plates.

The cats looked very happy and satisfied. Their coats were glossy, their eyes bright and intelligent, their whiskers spruce and clean.

They purred as they watched the little old man and Gobbolino heard their purring through the windowpanes.

"They look very content and well cared for," thought Gobbolino. "But nobody who has so many cats already can possibly want another."

He jumped lightly off the windowsill, but not before the little old man had seen him, for the next minute the door into the street opened wide and a voice called:

"Pussy! Pussy! Pretty pussy! Come here!"

"Oh, my goodness!" said Gobbolino. "He really is calling me!"

The little old man stood at the door with a piece of cat's-meat in his hand. He picked up Gobbolino and carried him into the room where all the cages were.

"There, my pretty!" said the little old man,

setting him down on the table. "Oh, what a pretty cat you are! And what beautiful blue eyes you have!"

Gobbolino did not very much like being prodded and poked by the little old man's hard, bony hands. His paws were felt, his teeth examined, his whiskers counted, and his tail measured.

"Oh, what a beautiful cat you are!" the little old man said over and over again.

The other cats looked on, sitting on their velvet cushions and growling with jealousy. They had finished their cat's-meat, and all the blue china saucers were licked clean.

When he had finished poking and prodding Gobbolino, the little old man popped him into an empty cage with another blue velvet cushion in it and a saucerful of cat's-meat.

Gobbolino would have preferred to sit by the fire, but he was grateful to the little old man for taking him in, so he ate up his cat's-meat thankfully and said nothing at all.

"It's nice to know there are such kind people in the world!" thought Gobbolino, as he sat on his velvet cushion. "For I might have been walking all night, or have starved to death."

"I'm sure I shall be very happy here," he said presently to his neighbour, a stately Persian madam. "But what are we all doing in these cages?"

"Don't you know?" said the Persian scornfully. "Why, you are now a show cat!"

In the morning the little old man brushed and combed his cats one by one till their fur gleamed and shone.

He was a little surprised at the coloured

73

sparks that flew from Gobbolino's coat under the brush, but he did not stop praising him or telling him how beautiful he was.

"Such fur! Such a tail! Such colouring! And such beautiful blue eyes!" he exclaimed.

The other cats growled in their cages, for they did not like to hear the little old man praising Gobbolino.

"Ha! They're jealous!" said the little old man, and tied a red ribbon round Gobbolino's neck to make him smarter than ever.

Every morning Gobbolino was brushed and combed with the other cats, till his coat shone and gleamed as theirs did, his eyes were as bright, and his whiskers as spruce and clean.

Every morning the little old man praised and admired him from the tip of his tail to his beautiful blue eyes, while the other cats growled jealously in their cages; they would not make friends with Gobbolino.

One day the little old man was especially busy, combing his cats, brushing the velvet cushions and polishing the cages from dark till dawn. He became very bad-tempered with his haste and exertion, scolding and hustling the cats and never once telling Gobbolino how beautiful he was.

"What is all the fuss and fluster about?" Gobbolino timidly asked his neighbour, the Persian madam.

"Don't you know?" she said scornfully. "Why, tomorrow is the Cat Show Day, and we are all going. That's what it is all about."

Gobbolino was quite excited to hear they were to have a change, for to tell the truth he had grown a little tired of his gilded cage and blue velvet cushion. He was very grateful to the little old man for giving him good food and a comfortable home, but sometimes he dreamed of a shabby rug before the fire, a cracked saucer of skim-milk, and the noisy chatter of children instead of the rows of cages, the proud unfriendly cats, the hours of brushing, and the bony hands of the little old man who poked and prodded him every morning, saying:

"Oh, what a handsome little cat you are! And what beautiful blue eyes you have!"

"But I am very ungrateful!" Gobbolino told himself, sitting upright on his velvet cushion. "For I might still be wandering homeless in the cold, and here I am, well fed and cared for, sitting on a velvet cushion – Gobbolino the show cat!"

Early the next morning the little old man

began to take down the cages, one by one, and pile them on to a little cart drawn by a scraggy pony.

Gobbolino's cage was put on the very top of all; he had a splendid view as they trotted along the countryside towards the show.

The Cat Show was held in the Town Hall, and long before they arrived, Gobbolino could hear the excited mewing of hundreds and hundreds of show cats.

There they were, in hundreds and hundreds of cages lining the Town Hall – big cats, little cats, black cats, white cats, tabby cats, Persian cats, fat cats, thin cats, handsome cats, ugly cats, cats from China, cats from Siam, Manx cats, pet cats, wild cats, tomcats, and last of all the little old man's cats, and Gobbolino the witch's kitten with his beautiful blue eyes looking on at it all.

"Oh, my goodness!" he said to himself as he looked at all the cats sitting on velvet cushions of every colour under the rainbow. "Whoever will notice any of us among such splendid company?"

For the little old man had told them he expected them all to win prizes, and especially Gobbolino. He had even threatened, if they did not, to stop their cat's-meat and to take away their velvet cushions, especially Gobbolino's. He had promised to cuff all their ears, and to turn them out into the street to look after themselves as best they might, particularly Gobbolino.

The little cat's heart sank as he saw all the splendid cages and thought of the little old man's words, for nobody would look at him among such splendid company.

But the other cats sat up proud and bold. They were all certain of winning prizes, whatever Gobbolino might say.

They began to talk to their neighbours, and whispers ran from cage to cage.

"Tell me, madam, who is that black and odd-looking stranger you have brought with you? I don't think I saw him here last show."

A silky chinchilla was speaking to the Persian who had been Gobbolino's neighbour before.

"No, master adopted him lately," the Persian replied. "We don't know much about him. To tell you the truth . . ." she began to whisper and Gobbolino could not hear what she said, nor what, in her turn, the chinchilla whispered to her neighbour, till a kind of hiss was running the round of the cages, with a murmuring echo:

"*Gobbolino! Gobbolino! Gobbolino!*"

Gobbolino took no notice. He did not know why the cats disliked him, or why they should be jealous of him, as the little old man said they were. He felt sure they were all twenty times more handsome than himself. He wished them no harm, and if they chose to whisper about him among themselves, he did not mind.

The judges went round among the cages, looking at the cats, examining and judging.

They went away and came back again, after which the little old man gave each cat a small piece of liver, and went to sleep on a sack behind the cages.

Presently the judges brought round coloured cards and pinned them on the cats.

The Persian had a red one with "First Prize" written on it. The chinchilla opposite had only a blue one: she was so jealous she turned her back and would not look at the Persian till her master took her away.

Some of the other cats had coloured cards as well – red, yellow, and blue ones. The little old man trotted among his cages, well pleased, stroking the heads of his prize-winners and promising them all kinds of good things for supper.

Gobbolino was delighted to see how many prizes they would carry home in the shabby little cart. He had not even noticed that his own cage held no prize-card at all, when the chief judge stood up to announce the name of the champion – the best cat in the show.

It was Gobbolino.

For a moment there was a great silence, and then a murmuring ran through the Town

Hall that rose to a hissing. It came from the cages.

The hissing grew to a spitting, and the spitting to a yowling.

In vain the judges tried to quell the noise, in vain the owners rattled on the cages or covered them with rugs – the angry cats yowled on and on, till one great voice arose from every cage announcing:

"But Gobbolino is a witch's cat!"

The judges turned pale, so did the owners.

The cat-fanciers, who had come to buy, looked at each other in horror, for each of them had been ready to offer the little old man large sums of money for Gobbolino.

The little old man himself, crimson with fury, shook his fist at the judges, and then at Gobbolino, while round and round the cages ran the angry murmur:

"*Gobbolino is a witch's cat!*"

"Oh, my goodness!" said Gobbolino, cowering on the blue velvet cushion in a corner of his cage. "Why was I born a witch's cat, oh why? I don't want to win prizes!" he sobbed. "I don't want to be a champion and have people admire me! I only want a friendly home with kindly people, that's not very much to ask. But oh, my goodness! What is going to happen to me now?"

He was not left long in doubt, for the angry judge turned on the little old man and ordered him to leave the Town Hall immediately. His cats were all disqualified, and especially Gobbolino. The little old man was bundled out into the street with all his cages, and at the last moment the judges sent his prize-cards after him. Perhaps after all, they said, he had not known he was showing a witch's cat.

But the little old man's rage was not cooled by saving his prize-cards.

He opened the door of Gobbolino's cage and dropped him out into the road.

"Miserable creature!" he raged. "Look what trouble you have brought upon me! Why didn't you tell me you were a witch's kitten? Be off with you directly and let me never see a whisker of your face again!"

He whipped up the scraggy pony and galloped away in a cloud of dust, with the cats' cages rocketing and banging, and the cats peering and mocking over their shoulders at Gobbolino.

He was not sorry to see the last of them, or to stretch his paws, which had become very cramped and stiff from sitting so long on a velvet cushion.

He was very sorry to have brought such trouble upon the little old man, but he had not really enjoyed being a show cat, and living in a cage had become very irksome and monotonous.

"I am sure there is a home not far away where I shall be welcome," thought Gobbolino.

10

GOBBOLINO AT SEA

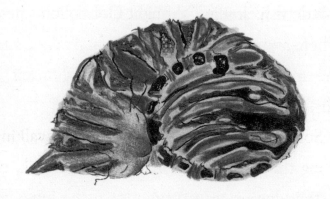

Gobbolino left the Town Hall far behind him and trotted steadily southward towards the sea.

He passed through towns and villages, past cottages and farmhouses, and small lonely dwellings, but every hearth had its tabby and every farm its brood of sleek mousers. There was no welcome anywhere for Gobbolino.

He kept himself from starving by killing rats in a rickyard, or mice in the hedges. He drank from the streams, where he sometimes caught a little fish, smiling to think of his clumsiness when, as an ignorant kitten, he had fallen into the millrace and nearly drowned himself – oh – ever so long ago it seemed today!

Sometimes he met a passer-by, walking along the road with a bundle on his back, or a stray dog or cat trotting down the highway on his own business, but they offered little companionship to Gobbolino.

Travellers had no hearth to share with him –

they gave him a friendly nod and tramped away. Dogs gave him one look of terror and ran for their lives, yelping madly till they reached their own kennels with their hair standing on end, while cats hissed savagely at him and would not answer the most civil greeting:

"Good morning, sister!"

"*Hiss-ss!*"

"It is a very fine morning, ma'am!"

"*Hiss-ss-ss!*"

"Can you tell me the way to the nearest village, my lady?"

"*Hiss-ss-ss-ss! Ss!*"

So that Gobbolino was lonely enough on his travels, and no wonder that his heart bounded to see the silver, sparkling sea, the ships lying at anchor with brown sails furled, distance making a pattern of their masts, and all the cheerful, busy life of the port.

Gobbolino trotted here and there among the boats, the bustling sailors, the women with their baskets, and the noisy, mischievous children, who were as eager as he to watch everything that was going on.

Nobody took any notice of a little cat, but there was a feeling of companionship in the stir and bustle, and Gobbolino did not hurry away, but sat on the quay in the yellow sunshine watching the ships and the gulls and the sailors on the decks below.

Presently a mouse ran out of a pile of ropes, and with a deft pat of his paw Gobbolino killed it. He was hungry, and his mother Grimalkin had taught him to be a good mouser.

"That was very neatly done, my friend!" said a voice behind him, and there was a pleasant-faced sailor boy standing and watching him with a kindly smile.

"There are plenty of mice on my ship, the *Mary Maud*!" said the sailor. "And we have no kitten at present. Would you like to come and catch them for us?"

Gobbolino's blue eyes shone with gratitude and joy.

"Oh, my goodness, my luck has changed at last!" he said to himself, while he thanked the sailor kindly and prepared to go with him. "Here is somebody who really wants me and needs me at last. I am sure I shall be very happy at sea – Gobbolino the sailor cat!"

When Johnnie Tar, the sailor, strode on board his ship, the *Mary Maud*, with Gobbolino under his arm, he received a great welcome from his mates. The cat was passed from horny hand to horny hand, petted, and made so much of that his heart nearly overflowed with joy.

"What a lucky cat I am!" said Gobbolino. "There was I, two hours ago, homeless, unwanted, unloved, and here I am, fondled and cared for by all the crew, from the captain to the cabin-boy. I have only to kill all the mice in the ship, to show them how grateful I am, and I shall certainly be very happy at sea. Perhaps, after all, I shall end my days on board this good ship *Mary Maud*!"

And indeed Gobbolino was as happy as any cat could be in the days which followed.

Though his heart sank somewhat when the ship put out to sea, and his beautiful blue eyes filled with tears at the thought of the miles of ocean that now lay between him and the little brothers he had come to love so dearly, yet the life was so free and pleasant, the sailors so kind and merry, and the whole atmosphere so full of goodwill and honest charity, that before many days had passed Gobbolino had come to look on the *Mary Maud* as his own home, and everyone aboard her as his close companions.

He cleared the ship of mice before she was out of sight of land. Those that he did not destroy jumped overboard in terror at the sound of his paws on the deck above.

"Here comes Gobbolino the mouser!"

He ran a thousand errands for the sailors, and, when there was nothing better to do, shared the watches with the look-out man, or paced the bridge side by side with the Captain, listening to age-old tales of the seven seas. All these he learned by heart so that he could repeat them to the little brothers on the happy day when he would be united with them again.

So they sailed on through sunny oceans, past yellow islands covered with palms, past coral reefs and lagoons so clear that the coloured fishes seemed to be lying on the top of the water watching the *Mary Maud* as, with her great brown sails spread to catch the breeze, she moved sedately past them on her journey round the world.

Happy, happy life for Gobbolino, who began to forget he had ever been born a witch's cat.

One fine morning Gobbolino sat in the prow looking out to sea, when a sudden shadow came over the sun, and a ripple of wind sent a hundred catspaws chasing down the calm blue sea.

Gobbolino shivered a little and turned round; sure enough, the shadow of a sea witch was crossing the sun, and although Gobbolino had never seen a sea witch before something told him that she was looking for trouble.

None of the sailors saw her flying up the sky, but they looked uneasily at the horizon.

"The wind is changing!" they muttered and began to reef in the sails.

By nightfall a storm was raging, and the waves were mountains high. The *Mary Maud* plunged up and down, while the wind shrieked in her rigging, and her timbers creaked and groaned.

The seas rose like pinnacles, curled over, and crashed on the decks, so that twice Gobbolino was only saved by a sailor from being washed overboard, and presently they carried him downstairs and locked him in the bo'sun's cabin, for none of them wanted to see their pet cat drowned.

It was safe and warm in the cabin and not unpleasant. Gobbolino curled up and went to sleep to the sound of the howling storm, the creaking and groaning of the *Mary Maud*.

"It will soon be over," said Gobbolino. "After all, one is bound to meet bad weather at sea, and the sooner I get used to it the better."

So whenever one of the kindly crew found time to shout through the cabin door:

"Are you there alive and hearty, Gobbolino?"

He answered:

"Ay, ay, mate!" in as cheerful a tone as he could muster and, closing his eyes, tried to imagine himself back in the warm farmhouse, or in the little brothers' nursery, or even sitting outside the witch's cave with his sister Sootica, telling each other all that they meant to do when they grew up.

The storm grew louder and fiercer, and the poor ship trembled as each wave struck her. Once there was a tremendous crash as though a mast had fallen on the deck and always there were the shouts of the sailors – too busy now to come and ask Gobbolino if he were still alive and hearty – the wail of the wind and the groan of the weary timbers.

"Oh, my goodness!" said Gobbolino as he was rolled from side to side. "Will it never come to an end, never? Surely when the morning comes the waves will die down, and the sea will be as calm and as beautiful as it was before."

But the morning came with the storm still raging, and now Gobbolino heard a new noise, the song of the sea witch as she flew round and round the ship:

"I'll send her down, the *Mary Maud*,
And every man of her aboard,
For not a sailor here can tell
The way to break a witch's spell!"

When he heard these words Gobbolino sat up
suddenly with his ears a-prick.

An old, old memory had stirred in him with
the sea witch's words.

Long, long ago, as he lay in the gloom of the
witch's cave with his little sister Sootica beside
him, their eyes scarcely opened, their paws
still pink and flat, he had heard his mother
Grimalkin and her mistress, the witch, talking
together.

"There is only one way to break a witch's
spell!" the witch had said. "You must pounce
on her shadow, stand on her head and cry the

words *'Fiddlesticks to you, ma'am!'* before she whisks her shadow away. No spell is proof against this counter-witchcraft."

When Gobbolino remembered this advice he grew quite crazy with excitement, and began to mew pitifully at the door, imploring the sailors to let him out.

For a long while nobody heard him, and when they did they quite refused to open the door.

"No, no, Gobbolino, the wind would blow you away, the waves would wash you overboard and the spray drown you. We cannot allow that. Stay where you are, and by and by when the storm is over we will let you out."

"But I'm so frightened down here!" complained Gobbolino, trying to make his voice sound as piteous as possible.

"It is ten times more frightening up here," said the sailor.

"I am so cold down here!" said Gobbolino.

"It is ten times colder up here!" said the sailor.

"I am so hungry down here!" sobbed Gobbolino.

"Well, I will see if I can find something for you to eat, if it has not all been washed away," said the kind-hearted sailor, "but you must wait here like a good cat until I come back again."

Gobbolino waited. As he listened to the groaning ship and the shriek of the storm that grew ever louder and louder, he thought that every minute the *Mary Maud* must plunge to the bottom of the sea and be lost.

He could hear the sea witch singing her song over and over again as she circled the ship.

The sailors took her for a seagull, and her song for the cry of a bird, but to Gobbolino, born in a witch's cave, a witch was always a witch, however she disguised herself, and he trembled to think of what she meant to do to the *Mary Maud* and all the sailors on board her.

When at last his kind friend returned with a morsel of fish and some milk in a tin, Gobbolino could hardly wait for him to unfasten the door. He slipped between the sailor's legs as the honest man stooped to lay the food before him, and was up on the deck in a flash.

"The cat has escaped!" the sailors cried who saw him, but the *Mary Maud* was near her end, and no one could spare a hand from the ropes to grab at Gobbolino.

To his surprise he found they were not far

from the shore, but the ship was running fast for a cruel-looking reef of rocks, and once she crashed on these there would be no hope left for her.

The night was gone and it was broad morning, but great clouds covered the sun, and where there was no sun there was no shadow for Gobbolino to jump upon. What is more, the sea witch flew aft the ship, as if she felt the danger of casting her shadow on it, and unless he could coax her nearer at the same time as the sun came out, the *Mary Maud* and all aboard her would be lost.

Gobbolino had to cling with all his might to the ropes and sails to avoid being washed into the sea, but at last he found a more sheltered spot where the wind and water could not reach him, though showers of spray still drenched his fur and stung his eyes, alert to watch the passing of the sea witch.

Oh, joy! Oh, joy for Gobbolino, when all of a sudden the clouds rolled back, and the sun moved into a rift of clear blue sky that flooded the deck and bathed the battered ship in glory.

The sea witch circled out to sea, sweeping angrily past the *Mary Maud* as if the cheering light annoyed her. Gobbolino was afraid she meant to fly away altogether, for the ship was bound for the rocks and nothing could save her.

And the sailors had suddenly caught sight of the little cat crouching in his corner.

"Save the cat! Save the cat!" they cried. "Put him in a basket, and if we strike the rocks he may float to shore!"

They left the ropes and six or seven of them

ran to seize Gobbolino but he slipped out of their hands and leapt on to the cookhouse roof.

The cook, still busy with his pans in spite of the ship's rolling, put out a hand to pull him inside, but Gobbolino made a leap and gained the Captain's bridge. The Captain clutched him by the scruff of his neck. Gobbolino gave a wriggle, the ship plunged again, and they fell to the ground in a heap.

Gobbolino found his feet first and sprang up the remaining mast, up, up, up to the cross-trees, and there was not a man reckless enough to follow him there in such a tempest.

The sailors stood below wringing their hands, for they felt sure that at any moment their kitten would be flung into the sea, while the sea witch flew round the ship in ever-widening circles, and the next bank of storm clouds moved up to swallow the sun.

Even if the sea witch saw him crouching there in the rigging, it meant nothing to her that a small dark cat had been foolish enough to climb the mast with the ship breaking to pieces beneath him.

But Gobbolino could not let her vanish in this fashion:

"Mistress! Oh, mistress!" he cried above the storm. "Don't you know me? Have you never met Grimalkin my mother, nor Sootica my little sister, nor my mistress the witch who lived in the cavern under the Hurricane Mountains? Oh, mistress! Oh, mistress! It is Gobbolino, the witch's kitten, who is calling to you! For my mother's sake, don't leave me to drown on this miserable ship! Have mercy! Have mercy!"

The sea witch heard his pitiful cries and

wheeled suddenly, just as she was preparing to fly away out of sight.

"Is it true what you say?" she cried above the storm. "If you are really a witch's kitten, what are you doing on board this ship?"

"The sailors took me aboard!" piped Gobbolino. "I couldn't escape – how could I, so far from the shore?"

"Witch's kittens swim like seals!" said the sea witch suspiciously, creeping nearer and nearer the ship, but careful not to let her shadow fall upon the deck.

"It was so far to the shore, mistress, that I was afraid!" said Gobbolino, anxiously watching the bank of cloud drawing nearer and nearer the sun. "Oh, take me on your broomstick, kind mistress, and carry me back to the cave in the Hurricane Mountains! You would not let a witch's kitten die, kind mistress?"

"Jump into the sea and swim!" said the sea witch. "When the ship is gone down I will pick you up on my broomstick and take you home again."

"It is so far and so deep!" sobbed Gobbolino. "I am afraid! I am afraid!"

"And, oh, my goodness!" he thought to himself. "In one more minute the sun will be gone, and then nothing that I can do will save us!"

So he clung to the rigging with all his might and main, sobbing:

"Oh! Oh! Oh! The wind is pulling me off! I shall fall on the deck and be smashed into a thousand pieces, and what will my mother Grimalkin say, and my little sister Sootica, and my mistress the witch? I am falling! I am falling!"

"I will save you! Be ready to spring upon my broomstick as I pass!" cried the sea witch angrily as the ship wallowed once more into the depths of a wave, and the rim of the sun touched the bank of cloud.

Gobbolino crouched on the mast as the ship rose again, watching, watching the deck.

The anxious sailors, who had heard his pitiful mewing, but could not understand all that he said, stood watching, too, each one ready to plunge into the sea to save him if he should fall.

The sunlight began to fade.

"Oh, my goodness, if it is already too late!" said Gobbolino, and now he saw the cruel reef of rocks rearing to the ship's bows.

"Be ready!" shrieked the sea witch almost in his ear. "Spring!"

But as she passed him like a streak of summer lightning her shadow fell for one moment on the deck, and in that moment Gobbolino sprang, not on her broomstick, but right on to the shadow of her head, crying loudly:

"*Fiddlesticks to you, ma'am!*" – and with a shriek of rage the sea witch was gone.

"Traitor! Traitor!" she cried, as the wind swallowed her up and then a dead calm fell on the sea.

A ship's length from the reef the *Mary Maud* lay becalmed, as if at anchor. The last storm clouds raced northward while the sun shone out of a hot blue sky.

The sea sparkled like a still lagoon, and far below, Gobbolino could see brown weed moored to rock terraces, pretty fishes, crabs, and eels, as clearly as if they swam in an aquarium.

All traces of the storm were gone.

Gobbolino looked about him in bewilderment. The sailors, too, seemed dazed and uncertain – they gathered in little groups, talking uneasily and peeping at Gobbolino.

"It was no seabird, I tell you!" he heard them whisper. "It was a witch!"

"He was talking to her! I heard him plainly!"

"He said he was a witch's kitten! Can you believe it?"

"No wonder she followed the ship and would not let us alone! We mighty nearly perished, I can tell you!"

"The cat bargained with her to stop the storm, and who knows what he may have offered her in exchange?"

"He cried, '*Fiddlesticks to you, ma'am!*' or some such rubbish!"

"Ah! Who knows what that may mean to a witch's cat!"

So they stared suspiciously at Gobbolino, and when he walked towards them none of them stooped to pick him up, or stroked his head.

All night long the ship lay becalmed under a silver moon.

Gobbolino sat on the deck, lonely and sad, for the sailors were awkward with him, and nobody invited him to share their meal.

In the morning a little breeze sprang up, but not a sailor appeared on deck, or made any attempt to unfurl the sails.

At midday the Captain came up alone.

"Gobbolino, my little cat," he said kindly,

but with great solemnity, "I am afraid the time has come when we must part. My sailors refuse to put to sea until you leave the ship. They are afraid of fresh troubles coming upon them or the sea witch revenging herself upon the ship for your sake. There are captains, and there are ships, Gobbolino, who will not have a cat aboard, they think it is unlucky. The *Mary Maud* is not one of these. But a *witch's* cat – oh, no! That is quite a different thing!"

Gobbolino nodded and answered, "Ay, ay, Cap'n!" though his eyes filled with tears at the thought of leaving his kind friends and the ship he had come to look on as his home.

THE LITTLE PRINCESS

Gobbolino was very touched when the Captain himself rowed him ashore in the *Mary Maud*'s lifeboat.

The sailors, watching from the ship's side, gave him a friendly cheer as the boat ran on the silver sands and the little cat jumped out, but he could not look back and see the *Mary Maud* setting sail without him.

So he hurried bravely along, never once turning his head, and taking very little notice of where he was going, because he was so busy trying not to cry, until he found himself in what must have been a very large town indeed, for the streets were so full and so busy that there wasn't room even for a kitten as neat and agile as himself to walk in peace.

For a time he dodged in and out of legs and leapt from in front of wheels until at last, after an extra hard kick had landed on his ribs, he decided that it would be safer to continue his journey overhead.

With one leap he was on top of a high wall, another leap and he was among the chimneys. With a sigh of relief he set out to continue his journey along the housetops.

When he came to the very end of the town he popped down what he took for a drainpipe.

"This will take me down again!" said Gobbolino. "And once I am on the ground I can run off into the open country and find somewhere where I shall be more welcome than in this place."

But what he had taken for a rainwater pipe was really a royal chimney.

Gobbolino did not know it, but he had popped down one of the chimneys in the king's palace.

Down, down, down the dark and narrow chimney fell Gobbolino, like a round ball that became blacker and blacker as he swept away the soot.

Bump! He landed at the bottom, and shot out into an open room, in time to hear a little voice like silver bells saying:

"Oh! Oh! Oh! Whatever can be coming down the chimney?"

Gobbolino opened his beautiful blue eyes and looked about him. He was in the prettiest room he had ever seen, all white lace and pink ribbons.

Watching him from a white bed in the middle of the room was a little girl with golden curls upon which rested a tiny crown. Her pink quilt was littered with toys and dolls. There were games and books on her satin pillows, flowers in great clusters round her bed, but her little face was pale and sad, even when her blue eyes opened wide in surprise at seeing Gobbolino.

He knew in a moment that she must be a princess.

"Oh! Oh! Oh!" said the little princess. "It's a cat! It is a lovely cat with the most beautiful blue eyes I ever saw! Oh, dear little cat! Pretty little cat! Do come nearer so I can speak to you and stroke your soft fur! Come and tell me your name and how you came to fall down my nursery chimney!"

Her voice was so kind and so charming that Gobbolino jumped upon her bed at once, quite forgetting the sooty black paw-marks he left wherever he went.

"The town children were chasing me, Your Highness!" he exclaimed. "My name is Gobbolino!" And then, her little hand was so kind, and her voice so gentle, while his own heart was so lonely, that he began to tell her his whole story from beginning to end, and all the while the princess gently stroked his fur, saying "Oh!" and "Ah!" whenever he paused, till the tale was over, when she said:

"Oh, *poor* little Gobbolino! How could people be so stupid and cruel? I can't understand it at all! But you mustn't be lonely and sad any longer, because I want you to live with me now for ever and ever – you shall be Gobbolino the royal cat!"

At that moment the door opened and the princess's nurse came into the room.

She threw up her hands in horror at the sight of Gobbolino.

"Your Royal Highness! Your Royal Highness! However did that dirty little cat get on your bed?" she exclaimed. "I thought I shut all the doors! I thought I shut all the windows! And he can't possibly have come down the chimney!"

"He *did* come down the chimney!" said the little princess. "He is Gobbolino, and he is going to stay with me and be my cat for ever and ever."

"We'll see what your doctor says about that!" said the nurse tartly, whisking away the pink satin cover which was all covered with Gobbolino's paw-marks. "He is just on his way to see you now. I can hear him coming up the stairs."

The princess's doctor was round and rosy. He came into the room smiling like the sun, and in less than no time the little princess had persuaded him to allow Gobbolino to stay for ever and ever.

"I feel better already, with him beside me!"

she told him. "But if you send him away I shall certainly be worse."

"What about all those pretty toys, those dolls and games and picture books I ordered for you instead of medicine?" said the doctor. "Those didn't make you better."

"They weren't alive," said the little princess. "I was just as lonely all the time they were there as before they came!"

So Gobbolino stayed in the little princess's room day in and day out, and which of them was the happier it would be difficult to say.

"Oh, my goodness!" Gobbolino said to himself sometimes, as he sat in the window looking down on the busy street below. "Here am I, born in a witch's cave, shunned and despised by everyone, about to live for ever and ever in a royal palace! What would my mother say? And my sister Sootica? Oh, my goodness! Whoever would have believed it?"

He did all in his power to amuse the little princess and keep her happy, for she had lain ill so many weary years that she had almost forgotten how to feel well again, but now, as Gobbolino talked to her, told her stories, and went through his tricks for her, the colour began to creep back into her pale cheeks once more.

When he told her of the adventure of the little brothers in the Lord Mayor's coach:

"One day I shall ride in a coach again!" she cried.

When he told her of his friends, the crew of the *Mary Maud*:

"One day I, too, shall go to sea!" she said.

Gobbolino would sit long hours on the

windowsill telling her about what went on in the street below.

Sometimes musicians came round the corner, and when Gobbolino had described how well they played and how the crowds gathered to hear them, the little princess had them brought up to her nursery, where they played her the sweetest airs they knew.

Another day a performing bear came down the street, so clumsy and droll, and playing such merry pranks that Gobbolino nearly fell off the windowsill with laughter, and the little princess would not rest until the bear too, and its master, were brought up the stairs to her room, though her parents, the nurse, the servants, and even the doctor, did all in their power to prevent it.

Sometimes it was a flower-seller, with a

basket of yellow, pink, heliotrope, blue, all the colours of the rainbow, who was brought to the little princess's bedside, and sometimes an acrobat who stood on his hands and walked about the room, or a juggler that tossed a dozen balls in the air at once, and balanced dishes on his nose.

The days were never dull for the little princess now. The roses bloomed in her cheeks and her eyes sparkled.

Her doctor, her nurse, and her parents were delighted with her.

"Soon she will be running about again, and then she will be able to go to boarding-school like the other princesses," they said.

"Can I take Gobbolino with me when I go to school?" the little princess asked.

"Oh, no, of course not!" said her parents, her

nurse, and her doctor, looking quite shocked. "You will have so much to do there you will have no time to play with your cat!"

"Then I don't want to get better and go to school!" sobbed the little princess when she and Gobbolino were left together again. "I want to stay here in my nursery with you, and have fun together! I shan't get well after all!"

So the little princess refused her meals and lay on her back looking up at the ceiling.

She no longer asked for the singers, the performing animals, the acrobats and the jugglers to be brought up to her room as before. She wanted everyone to think she was very ill, or they would send her to school immediately.

But when her parents, the doctor, and the nurse were out of the room, the little princess sat up on her satin pillows and asked:

"What can you see in the street, Gobbolino?" and Gobbolino would reply:

"I can see a procession, Your Highness!" or "I can see a farmer going to market!" or "A circus!" or "A fair!" and the little princess would cry:

"Tell me all about it!"

But one day Gobbolino cried out all by himself:

"Oh! Oh! Oh! I can see a Punch and Judy show coming round the corner!"

"Tell me all about it! Tell me all about it!" cried the little princess, but Gobbolino was so doubled up with laughter at the antics of the cherry-nosed Punch, the policeman, and the dog Toby that he could not speak fast enough to please her, and at last the little princess skipped out of bed, ran across the room, and knelt on the window seat beside him where she began to split her sides, crying:

"Oh! Oh! Oh! I'd rather belong to a Punch and Judy show than anything in the world!"

Gobbolino and the little princess were so busy clapping their hands at the Punch and Judy show, shouting:

"Hurray! Hurray! Hurray!" and bouncing up and down, that they did not hear the door open behind them, until a whole chorus of voices exclaimed:

"Princess! Princess! Your Highness! Your Highness! What is the meaning of all this?" and there on the threshold stood the princess's parents, her nurse, her doctor, and all the palace servants, staring with astonishment into the room.

The little princess skipped back to bed and drew the bedclothes over her head.

"Did you see that?" said her parents.

"She is perfectly well!" said her nurse.

"There is nothing whatever wrong with her!" said the doctor, and they all added:

"She must go to boarding-school at once!"

"I don't feel well at all!" sobbed the little princess, but nobody believed her any longer.

The very next morning she was packed into her father's coach and galloped away to boarding-school with a dozen or so other princesses, where I feel bound to tell you she was very happy indeed.

She had only time to fling her arms round Gobbolino's neck before she went.

"Goodbye, my dear, darling, little cat!" she said. "How lucky you are, Gobbolino! You can go anywhere in the wide world that you please, but look at me!"

"I don't know where to go," said Gobbolino, with tears standing in his beautiful blue eyes at the thought of being alone in the world once more.

"Why don't you join the Punch and Judy show?" said the little princess. "That's what I would do if I were free."

At that moment she was bundled into her father's coach with all her boxes and trunks, and before long a cloud of dust hid them all from view.

Gobbolino sat on the nursery windowsill watching the coach until it disappeared with the princess's tiny white handkerchief still fluttering from the window.

The nursery seemed so empty and silent without her, he did not care to stay even a night longer in the king's palace, but slipped silently down the stairs and out into the street the first time the door was opened.

12
PUNCH AND JUDY

Gobbolino left the town as quickly as possible and trotted down the country lanes.

Often he stopped a passer-by to ask politely:

"Please, sir, or ma'am, can you tell me, has a Punch and Judy show passed this way?" and often he had the answer:

"Why, yes, my little cat. I saw it playing on the village green back yonder. You will certainly catch it up if you trot fast enough."

And Gobbolino trotted as fast as his paws would carry him to the next village and the next and the next.

At the entrance of every village he was sure to ask:

"Please, has a Punch and Judy show been here lately?"

And he always had the answer:

"Why, yes, my little cat, it was here only yesterday. You will certainly catch it up if you trot fast enough."

At last in the distance he saw a crowd

gathered under a tree, and there sure enough was the striped show-box, and the gaudy figures of Punch and Judy.

But they were not playing today to an eager crowd. The show-people sat around sad and despondent. Some bent their heads on their hands, while others stared into the distance, saying nothing at all. It was a pitiful sight to behold, and Gobbolino lost no time in asking a woman on the outskirts of the crowd what the matter could be, and whether he could give them any help in their distress.

"Our dog Toby has died!" the woman told him, wiping away a tear. "And of course Punch and Judy cannot perform without him. We shall all be ruined."

"Oh dear! Oh dear! That is very sad!" said Gobbolino with much sympathy. "I was just about to join your show and travel the country with you, but I see now I shall hardly be wanted since there is not a show any longer."

The woman looked him up and down. Then she called the showman, who was gloomily mending a rent in the show-box.

"Dandy! Dandy? Come here and look at this kitten! He talks of joining our show. Why shouldn't he take Toby's place and go along with us? With a ruff round his neck, who is to notice? Only a black face instead of a white, and such beautiful blue eyes! He may save our fortunes yet!"

Dandy the showman stared at Gobbolino and finally said:

"Well, why not? He looks pretty enough and clever enough, and if we have no Toby we shall be ruined. Will you do your best for us, little cat with the blue eyes, if we give you a home in our company?"

"That I will gladly, master!" said Gobbolino in delight, so the showman's wife dressed him up in a paper ruff and a blue jacket and popped him into the striped show-box with Punch and Judy and the policeman and the baby.

At first these were very ready to be jealous of him and to dislike him, but when they saw how modest Gobbolino was, how sweet-tempered, and how eager to ask: "Should Dog Toby act like this? Or like this?" they soon became friendly in return, and it was the gayest company in the land that set forth again presently to entertain the next village they could find.

Crowds gathered the moment that the striped show-box came into sight:

"Here's the Punch and Judy! Here's the Punch and Judy!"

Dandy the showman would halt on the village green and set up the box; soon Punch and Judy were at their tricks and the crowd were roaring with laughter, but it was always the dog Toby who was asked for again and again: "Toby! Toby! Show us Dog Toby! Oh, what a clever fellow he is, and what beautiful blue eyes he has!"

Gobbolino acted so well and entered into his part so eagerly that there was always a whole capful of silver at the end of the show.

The showman's children had new shoes, his wife wore bracelets, and the showman himself wore a yellow waistcoat.

"And all thanks to you, my little friend!" he would say affectionately, rubbing Gobbolino under the ears. "What do you say to joining the show for good – eh? A cat might have a worse home, after all."

"I will gladly stay with you for ever, kind master!" Gobbolino replied at once, for strange as were his new surroundings after the luxury of the palace, he found his new life as pleasant as he could wish for.

He enjoyed watching the crowds gather as the striped Punch and Judy went from village to village. He enjoyed the grins that widened on the children's faces when he and Punch popped up in the box. He loved to see the careworn faces of the old men and women, the worried faces of mothers, break into smiles as they forgot their troubles in following his tricks.

"Really there is nothing so pleasant as

making people happy!" said Gobbolino. "I shall be perfectly content to stay here for ever – Gobbolino the performing cat."

He often wished the little princess could watch his acting. He had secret hopes that one day the showman might find his way to the boarding-school, or to the orphanage gates, or even to the nursery of the little brothers, and meanwhile he was very happy, particularly in the evenings when the show-people put up their little tents round a blazing campfire and Gobbolino sat peacefully beside it, his paws tucked under his chest, as content as the sleekest tabby on a kitchen hearth.

"At last I have found my home!" he said to himself. "Who would ever have believed it would be such a strange one? But what matter? For here I am."

One day they came to a village that was less pleasant than the rest.

The houses were grey and dirty. No flowers grew in the gardens, which were full of weeds. The street was littered with rubbish, while the pond on the village green was thick with duckweed and slime.

Nobody came out to greet the Punch and Judy show when the showman put up his striped box on the green.

A few children, slouching home from school, stared rudely but went home to tell their parents, for just as the showman was about to move on, a few people began to straggle up and stood about in little groups to watch the show.

The showman would willingly have left such disagreeable people behind, but being a merry-hearted man himself, he thought he had better do all he could to cheer their misery, so he set Gobbolino beating a drum and drew up the curtain.

The children and their parents watching did not clap their hands as most children did.

Instead, they began to make rude remarks.

"Punch has cracked his nose! Judy's pinny is torn! Look at Toby's face! Whoever saw a black dog Toby before?"

"The old show-box could do with a clean! And the showman too, I daresay!"

"And Dog Toby, he's black enough!" shouted someone else.

All the children laughed, but it was very disagreeable laughter.

Suddenly a voice from the back called out:

"That isn't a dog at all! It's a cat!"

Gobbolino bristled all over with rage, and the voice called out again:

"It's a cat, I tell you! And what is more it is a witch's cat, or I am very much mistaken!"

The crowd turned round to stare at the ugly old crone who stood at the back, leaning on her stick and croaking out her words with an ugly leer.

"Old Granny Dobbin ought to know! She's a witch herself!" cried the children in chorus.

The showman began to pull down the little curtain to close the show, but the children would not be quieted.

"A witch's cat! A witch's cat!" they sang. "Take off his ruff and let us see the witch's cat!"

They made a path for old Granny Dobbin and pushed her to the front.

"Speak to the witch's cat, Granny!" they

shouted. "Make him speak to you! Make some magic for us!"

"Ha! Ha!" croaked the old woman, pointing her finger at Gobbolino. "I know you! Grimalkin was your mother! Your little sister Sootica is apprenticed to a witch, way up in the Hurricane Mountains! *You* a dog Toby, indeed! Ho! Ho! Ho!"

The fathers and mothers of the children, standing behind, grew threatening, and shook their fists at the showman.

"How dare you bring a witch's kitten into our village?" they cried. "How dare you harm our children so? They might be turned into mice, or green caterpillars, or toads! If it hadn't been for old Granny Dobbin here, goodness knows what might have happened! Away with you directly!"

"Out of the village! Chase them out of the village!" clamoured the children, picking up sticks and stones, and they all became so angry and pressing that the showman lost no time in packing up his box and preparing to depart.

Gobbolino, his ruff taken off, did all he could to explain himself to the angry villagers, but nobody would listen to him except old Granny Dobbin.

"It's no good, my poor simpleton!" she said when he had finished his story. "Nobody will ever keep you for long. Once a witch's cat, always a witch's cat. You will never find the home of your dreams while your eyes are blue and sparks come out of your whiskers."

"I have met plenty of kind people in the world!" said Gobbolino stoutly. "I feel sure that one day I shall find the home I am looking for."

"Never! Never! Never!" said the old hag. "Today or tomorrow you will realize I am telling you the truth! A kitchen hearth and a cosy fireside! Ha! Ha! Ha! That you will never know, witch's kitten!"

Gobbolino's beautiful blue eyes filled with tears, but there was no time to stay and ponder over the witch's words, for the showman had shouldered his box and was striding up the village street with a pack of village children at his heels, all jeering and booing in the most unpleasant fashion.

They kept this up all the way to the next village, so that the showman dared not stop there, although it was quite a pleasant place, but had to trudge on all the weary miles to the next, by which time darkness had fallen and it was time to camp for the night.

It was pleasant to awaken to bright sunlight shining on whitewashed cottages and gardens gay with flowers.

The children were clean and rosy-cheeked in their pretty pinafores. The showman was surprised to see them hanging back as he set up his box on the green.

"Won't you come and look?" he invited them.

"We've heard you have a witch's cat instead of a dog Toby!" they told him, with their fingers in their mouths. "Our mothers said it would hurt us, and our fathers told us to go straight to school. We mustn't stop."

So they took hands and ran away. There was nobody left to watch the Punch and Judy, and soon the showman packed up again and went on his way.

It was the same at the next village, and the next and the next. The word had gone before, as swift as the wind, "The showman has a witch's cat!" and nobody would come to see.

"It is of no use, master!" Gobbolino said at last, when the seventh village had refused to look at them. "You will be ruined, I see, if I stay with you any longer. You must find a new dog Toby, and I must find a new home. I am sorry, dear master, I really am, for bringing such trouble on your head; but I did not choose my birthplace, and sorrow enough it has brought me. Goodbye and good luck to you, master dear. And may your fortune mend quickly!"

The honest showman, with tears running down his cheeks, agreed at last that Gobbolino was right. He embraced the little cat very fondly, and when Gobbolino had said a sad goodbye to all the show-people he watched them trudge away in a little cloud of dust without him.

"Oh, why was I born a witch's cat? Oh, why?" thought Gobbolino when at last they were out of sight. "I could wish for nothing better than a home with such kind and pleasant people as these, but no! Everyone turns against me, and, oh, my goodness, what is to become of me now?"

13
GOBBOLINO IN THE TOWER

Gobbolino was sitting sadly by the roadside thinking of his hard fate when he heard the *Clop! Clop! Clop!* of an approaching horse and rider.

A white horse was coming along the king's highway, decked in gold and scarlet as a knight's horse should be, but for all this gay dress the knight who sat astride it was pale and wan. He gazed straight ahead of him so mournfully that Gobbolino's heart ached for him, and he quite forgot his own troubles.

The knight would have passed by without noticing the witch's kitten had not his horse suddenly shied, nearly throwing his rider, who became aware of Gobbolino, and looking kindly into his beautiful blue eyes said:

"Good-day to you, my little cat! What are you doing in the king's highway? Surely you are rather far from home?"

"I have no home, kind sir!" replied Gobbolino humbly. "I beg your pardon for getting in your way, but I was wondering how best to find one."

"You are a very pretty cat!" the knight said, stooping to stare at Gobbolino. "And you have beautiful blue eyes and three very handsome black paws besides a white one. Tell me, do you think you could amuse a fair lady?"

"I am not very clever, but I could tell her stories," said Gobbolino, thinking of the tales he used to tell the little princess.

"Could you make her laugh and sing?" asked the knight.

"I am not very amusing, but I could play tricks on her!" replied Gobbolino, thinking of the pranks he had played on the farmer's children and on the little brothers.

"Could you make her fall in love with a humble knight?" the knight asked very sadly.

"I could put her under a spell," said Gobbolino, remembering the magic he had learned in the witch's cave. He wished with all his heart to help this kind knight with the sad eyes, who spoke to him so gently.

"Then I think you will do very well as a present for my lady fair," said the knight, holding out his foot to Gobbolino. "Jump upon my horse and come with me!"

Gobbolino sprang lightly on to the knight's foot and then on to the saddle, and they rode away together in a cloud of dust.

While they rode, the knight told Gobbolino the cause of his sadness.

He was in love with a beautiful lady who had been shut up in a tower by her father until she should make up her mind which of two suitors she would marry. One was the sad knight himself, and the other the black baron who lived in a castle nearby.

Both of them went to visit her every day and took her presents, and each of them tried to bring her something that would please her better than the other.

Every day when he came, the black baron would guess what present the sad knight had brought the day before, and he was always right. Every day the sad knight tried to guess what present the black baron had brought her. And he never made a mistake either.

The fair lady, whose name was Alice, had laughingly promised to marry the suitor whose present the other could not guess.

The sad knight had brought lilies, roses, jewels, and a nightingale in a golden cage – and the black baron had guessed them all.

The black baron had brought a silver swan, lovebirds, rare fruits, and a musical box – and the sad knight had never failed to find out any of them.

Neither of them had ever thought of a little black cat with three black paws and beautiful blue eyes.

The tower stood in the middle of a wood. It was guarded by a dragon, but he was old and lazy, and he always let the knights go by.

Gobbolino had never seen a dragon before, and he was more than a little frightened when the trees opened out into a grassy sward, the tower rose before them, and he saw the green coils of the monster lying about its foundations. The knight jumped boldly from his horse, however, and thundered on the door of the tower, holding Gobbolino on his arm.

The dragon opened one eye and looked at them, but it did not move, and a little serving maid, the Lady Alice's only attendant, tripped down the stairs and opened the door.

"Is my lady alone?" the knight asked her.

"Why, yes, Sir Knight," said the little maid. "The baron departed half an hour ago, having brought my lady the loveliest set of ivory balls you ever saw! She heard your horse splashing across the ford, and is waiting to receive you."

Gobbolino was no longer surprised that the suitors found it so easy to guess each other's presents, and he made up his mind that the baron should not find out so quickly about himself.

The knight and Gobbolino followed the little maid up the winding stair to the top where the Lady Alice sat beside her spinning-wheel and looked out over the forest.

The moment she saw Gobbolino she cried out:

"Oh, what a pretty little cat! Oh, do let him come and sit on my lap, so I may tickle his ears!"

Gobbolino leapt lightly on to her lap and sat there purring, while the fair lady rubbed his chin gently with her long white fingers and her rings played a hundred tunes in his ears.

"Stay with me for ever, little cat!" the Lady Alice whispered. "It is so lonely here in the tower with nobody but my serving maid and these stupid knights and that lazy fat dragon to talk to."

"I will stay with you willingly, madam," Gobbolino replied, for he was always anxious to please and to make people happy. Besides, he could think of worse homes than the tower in the forest, with a fair lady to tickle his ears and all the wide woods and trees to behold around him. If he could cheer the Lady Alice's solitude a little he felt he would be willing to make his home with her for ever.

The knight was highly pleased to see Lady Alice so delighted with his present.

"I have never had such a pretty gift before!" said she.

"What about the gift my friend the black baron brought you earlier in the day?" said the knight slyly.

"Oh, that!" said Lady Alice. "Yes, it was very pretty indeed, but it hadn't such sleek black fur, such dainty paws and such beautiful blue eyes!"

"I wonder what it can have been?" said the

knight, pretending to be very puzzled.

"I wonder, indeed!" returned the lady with her eyes full of laughter.

"Not a goldfish, I suppose?" said the knight.

"Oh, no! No! No! What amusement should I find with a goldfish in this tower? I wouldn't thank him for a goldfish!"

"Not a pot of ferns?" said the knight.

"Oh, no! No! No! My little serving maid can bring me all the ferns I want out of the forest. I wouldn't thank him for a pot of ferns."

"Then it was not, I suppose, a set of ivory balls?" suggested the knight.

"Why, yes, it was!" said the lady, clapping her hands. "How clever you are to be sure! I shall have to tell the baron I cannot marry him after all, since you have guessed his present."

"He will never guess *mine*!" said the knight,

looking at Gobbolino. "And then you will have to marry *me*!"

"We shall see! We shall see!" said Lady Alice, gently stroking Gobbolino's fur.

When he left the tower the knight pressed a silver coin into the hand of the little serving maid and whispered:

"Don't tell the baron of my present, Rosabel!" and the little serving maid dipped a curtsey as she meekly replied:

"Oh, no, Sir Knight, that I never will!"

Gobbolino passed the rest of the day telling stories to the Lady Alice. He found her kind, and as bored as the little princess. She listened with interest to the tales he told, and laughed aloud when he blew coloured sparks out of his ears and hid himself in odd places round the tower.

The little serving maid peeped through the door and laughed too, while purple shadows crept over the forest, the stars came out, and Lady Alice pulled her harp close to the fire and began to sing.

Sitting at her feet, Gobbolino thought he had never been so contented before.

"How strange this is!" he said to himself. "Here am I, born in a witch's cave, turned out of an orphanage, betrayed by a sea witch, the plaything of a little princess, come to end my days after all in a tower in the middle of a forest, guarded by a dragon. But it suits me very well, and if every evening is as pleasant as this one I shall be happy to remain for ever Gobbolino the prisoner cat."

But out of loyalty to the knight he did not want the black baron to guess his present, so when the next morning Lady Alice leaned out of her tower window and cried:

"I can see the baron crossing the ford! Go down and let him in, Rosabel, and mind you do not let him know what present the knight has brought me!"

Gobbolino, who guessed that the little serving maid had broken her promises before, slipped out of the room behind her and hissed in her ear:

"If you tell the baron about me, Rosabel, I will turn you into a gingerbread doll, and the dragon will eat you up!"

"Oh, my! Oh, my!" shrieked the little maid in terror, running down the stairs.

Gobbolino had never threatened anyone before and he did not know if he really could turn anyone into a gingerbread doll if he tried. He felt very ashamed of himself as he trotted back to his fair mistress and crept under her couch.

"I didn't mean it," he said to himself. "I wouldn't hurt her for the world. Bad will out, I suppose. It comes of being born a witch's cat."

The black baron thundered on the tower door, and the little serving maid opened it, but she would not say a word about the present the knight had brought the Lady Alice. The baron came up the stairs in a very bad temper, for Rosabel had never failed to tell him before.

"Oh, no! No! No! I mustn't! I mustn't!" was all she would reply.

Lady Alice received the baron very graciously, but when he came to the knight's present she only closed her eyes and smiled.

"It wasn't a pair of pigeons, I suppose?" the baron asked.

"Oh, dear me, no! Just look at all the pigeons there are in the forest that come to my call!" said the Lady Alice scornfully.

"It wasn't a silver mirror?" the baron said.

"Oh, dear me, no! I have a bowl of crystal water from the spring that is better than any mirror," said Lady Alice. "When I smile into it the smile breaks into little ripples till all the water is laughing. *Ha! Ha! Ha! He! He! He!* I wouldn't thank him for a mirror!"

"It wasn't a little black rabbit to amuse you?" said the baron.

"Oh, no indeed!" said Lady Alice, but she turned just a little pale, and soon after the baron took his leave and went away.

If he did not guess in two more days the

Lady Alice would not marry him at all, and that would certainly please the knight.

The baron left behind him a handsome golden cockerel, but it crowed so loudly that the knight heard it far across the forest as he rode to the tower in the evening.

He was so sure that the baron could not guess his gift that he had not brought any other present, and so delighted that he gave the little serving maid two silver coins when he left and whispered:

"Now, mind you do not tell the baron anything about my present!"

"Oh, no, Sir Knight!" the little serving maid replied, but Gobbolino thought it as well to say the next morning:

"Remember if you say anything about my being here I shall turn you into a gingerbread doll, and the dragon will certainly gobble you up!"

"How terrible this is!" he said to himself as he crept under his mistress's gown. "Bad will out, I suppose, or I would not twice be threatening that little maid with such terrible revenge. But she is very heedless, I feel, and after all, I owe this kind home to the knight."

"Oh, my! Oh, my!" sobbed the little serving maid, flying down to open the door to the baron, and she would not breathe a word to him about the knight's present.

The baron came up the stairs in a passion. He guessed a silken gown, a lace pillow, and a jar of honey, all of which were wrong.

He threw his gift of roses on the floor and stamped down the stairs. When the knight came up later there were still petals clinging to the tapestry and of course he guessed at once what the baron had brought.

He was so sure of his own success that he had brought no other present, and he gave the little serving maid three silver coins when he went away.

"Now, don't you tell the baron of my present tomorrow," he said to her. "And by the evening Lady Alice will be mine."

But when night fell the Lady Alice brought out her harp while the little serving maid went down to wash the dishes. Gobbolino sat at his mistress's feet and listened, but the music grew sadder and sadder, till at last she burst into tears and, taking Gobbolino into her lap, laid her face against his fur and sobbed:

"Alas! Alas! What is to become of me? Tomorrow the baron will come for the last time, and when he fails to guess the knight's present I shall have to marry the knight. Certainly he is pleasant enough, but both are so stupid, I have no wish to marry either of them! I had far rather remain for ever in this tower and play my harp, my dear sweet little Gobbolino, until my true lover comes to find me! Once, long ago, I was in love with a noble young lord, but we were too young to marry and he left home to go to the wars. I have never seen him since, and now my father says I must marry one of these foolish suitors. Oh, Gobbolino! Gobbolino! What shall I do? What shall I do?"

Gobbolino was terribly distressed when he remembered how he had helped to bring about his mistress's downfall.

"It comes of being born a witch's cat," he told

himself. "Bad will out, I see. Now, if I had not threatened Rosabel, and let things take their course, the knight and the baron might have gone on guessing till the end of their days, and my fair lady would not have to marry either of them."

So he determined the next day to leave the tip of his tail exposed when he crept under the couch, so the baron would see him and guess what the present had been.

But before he could play this trick the baron had found out all for himself.

He arrived at the tower in the greatest state of excitement, for he knew that if he failed today, the Lady Alice would never be his.

In his hand he held five golden coins, for he was quite determined to bribe the little serving maid into telling him what the present had been.

Gobbolino had not said a word to her this morning, but she was far too frightened to open her mouth to the baron.

"Oh, no! No! No!" she sobbed. "Indeed I dare not; do not ask me, Baron, for pity's sake leave me alone!"

"But what can harm you, my poor child, if you just breathe one word to me?" asked the baron.

"Why, the present, Baron! The present can harm me!" cried Rosabel. "He had the fiercest look you ever saw when he threatened me!"

"Why, you do not mean to tell me that the present had a tongue?" asked the astonished baron.

"Why, yes, Baron, indeed it had a tongue,

and the brightest blue eyes you ever saw!" said the little serving maid directly. "And it said it would harm me severely!"

"Why, you don't mean to tell me the present had claws?" the baron asked.

"Why, yes, indeed it had, Baron, and the longest tail you ever saw!" said the little serving maid. "And the way it ran up and down the stairs in great bounds would astonish you! But it promised to put a spell on me if I told, and the look on its whiskers was so terrible, Baron, that I dare not disobey!"

"I have it!" shouted the baron. "It was a cat!"

"Oh, my! Oh! Oh! Oh!" sobbed the little serving maid in terror. "Now you have found out all about it by yourself! But it is a witch's cat, Baron, and very mischievous and harmful! I saw it blow sparks out of its ears! I saw it hide in my lady's shoe! It said it would turn me into a gingerbread doll and the dragon would eat me up! Oh! Oh! Oh! Whatever will become of us all?"

At that moment a second thundering knock shook the tower, and the knight arrived at the door.

He was so impatient to claim Lady Alice's hand that he could not wait till evening, but had arrived hard on the heels of the baron.

Both sprang up the stairs with the little maid sobbing between them and there sat Lady Alice with Gobbolino on her knee, for she had heard every word that went on below.

"It is a witch's cat!" shouted the baron.

"The serving maid betrayed me!" cried the knight.

"It will cast a spell on us all!" said the baron.

"I claim your hand, my lady!" said the knight, at which the baron drew his sword and they fell upon each other.

At that moment a bugle call sounded through the forest, and a white horse and rider came galloping across the ford.

The Lady Alice, who had been wringing her hands, gave one look from her window and tears of joy sprang into her eyes.

"It is he! It is my lord himself!" she cried and darted to the stairs.

The little maid followed her, jumped over the dragon's coils and ran sobbing towards her home at the edge of the forest, but Lady Alice ran to meet her young lover, who lifted her into his arms, placed her gently before him on the saddle, wheeled his horse round, and galloped back through the ford again with one last bugle call of triumph.

Gobbolino, half way down the stairs, saw them disappear in a cloud of dust, and his heart was happy for them.

He watched the pink frock of the little serving maid vanishing among the trees, and wished her well too, as she departed.

Upstairs the knight and the baron were still fighting when a rumbling as of an earthquake shook the tower.

The dragon was beginning to wake up.

The tower began to rock as he slowly uncoiled himself, and to totter as he stretched his claws one by one.

Then with a tremendous gape he opened his mouth and roared, and the bricks came tumbling down.

Stones, parapets, stairs, collapsed on top

of one another, and Gobbolino had barely time to leap clear himself when the whole tower crashed about his heels, bringing down the baron and the knight, still whirling their swords, among the ruins.

By the time they had picked themselves up, the dragon was crawling away to some peaceful cavern of his own in the forest.

Gobbolino decided to leave the place, too, so he trotted quietly into the shadow of the trees and disappeared.

14
GOBBOLINO THE WOODCUTTER

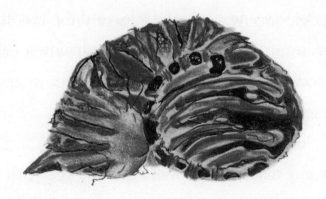

Night fell, and the loneliness of the forest fell on Gobbolino.

He was an easily pleased and independent

little cat, but company meant a great deal to him. He did not ask for much, only the murmur of friendly voices about him, the click of a knitting-needle, the bubble of a kettle, or the hiss of a cooking-pot.

Here, deep in the forest, the trees sighed as if they, too, missed the companionship of human beings, and Gobbolino, treading its gloomy ways, looked eagerly for the sign of some cottage or farmhouse, where the candlelight, shining through the windowpanes, might bid him welcome.

So it was with the greatest pleasure in the world that he saw, walking along the path in front of him, an aged woodcutter, quite bowed beneath a load of wood.

Gobbolino did not say a word as he joined him, but trotted silently at the woodcutter's heels, while a great peace came upon his heart, and the night fell softly around them.

The moon had risen when at last Gobbolino and the old man reached a tiny cottage, and not until he had thrown down his bundle of sticks on the doorstep did the woodcutter notice Gobbolino.

"Well! Well! Well!" exclaimed the woodcutter. "This is a surprise to be sure. And where did you come from, my pretty little cat?"

"I was just walking through the forest, master," Gobbolino explained. "The way was so long and so lonely, I was glad enough to fall in behind you. I hope you do not object."

"Well, you are perfectly right, the forest is very lonely," agreed the woodcutter, nodding his head. "Even an old man like me feels the need of company sometimes. My granddaughter is gone away, and I live all alone. What do you say to a place on my hearth and a saucer of milk in my kitchen? I can think of worse homes for a cat than mine!"

"Oh, master, master!" said Gobbolino, almost crying in his thankfulness and joy. "How can I thank you? Can it possibly be true that I have found a home at last – Gobbolino the woodcutter's cat?"

"Come in and see your new home, my little friend," said the woodcutter, opening the door, and Gobbolino trotted in at his heels.

What was his surprise to see a pink frock sitting on the hearth and above it the rosy cheeks and blue eyes of the little serving maid Gobbolino had last seen running through the forest!

"Granddaughter!" exclaimed the woodcutter in great astonishment. "What has happened? What are you doing here? Have you been dismissed?"

"Oh, no! No! No!" sobbed the little serving maid, beginning to cry bitterly.

"Such terrible things happened, grandfather, as you cannot imagine! The knights fought, the dragon roared, the tower fell down, and my Lady Alice rode away on a white horse! I was so frightened I jumped over the dragon and ran away. I have been running through the forest all day long to find you, grandfather!"

"Well, well, well!" said the woodcutter, patting her very kindly on the head. "All is well that ends well, for here you are safe at home, granddaughter, and no doubt we shall live together very comfortably as before. And just see what a pretty playfellow I have for you here, with such a splendid coat, such elegant paws, and such beautiful blue eyes!"

But his granddaughter screamed when she saw Gobbolino.

"Oh! Oh! Oh! Send it away! Send it away! That cat is the cause of all our troubles! It is no common tabby, but a witch's cat that blows sparks out of its whiskers, as I saw with my own eyes. Turn it out directly, grandfather, or I shall run straight out into the forest and never return!"

But the woodcutter picked up Gobbolino and set him gently on his knee.

"Tell me, my little cat," he said kindly. "Is this true what my granddaughter says about you?"

"Why, yes, master, it is," agreed Gobbolino sadly.

"And can you blow sparks out of your whiskers as my granddaughter says you can?"

"Why, yes, master, I can certainly do that," said Gobbolino.

"But you have never done anyone any harm, have you, my little cat?" the old man asked.

"Oh, no, master, never, never, never!" said Gobbolino, shaking his head. So, although his granddaughter sulked and stamped her foot and tossed her head, the woodcutter refused to turn Gobbolino out of doors, but poured him out a saucer of milk and gave him a comfortable corner beside the fire.

Now that she was home again, the woodcutter's granddaughter looked after the house, kept the kitchen spick and span, washed the dishes, and cooked the dinner while her grandfather worked in the forest.

"Stay at home with her and look after her!" the woodcutter said to Gobbolino. "I should not like any harm to come to her while I am away."

So Gobbolino stayed in the cottage, and although at first the girl tossed her head whenever she saw him, by and by, having no one else to talk to, she threw a remark or two at him while she wiped the pots and pans, till presently she was chattering merrily, and seemed to have forgotten her grudge against him.

"It was bad enough in the tower," she grumbled. "But there was my lady who talked to me, and knights who came every day, bringing such beautiful presents! My lady gave me all her old dresses to wear, but here I am with nothing at all but this patched gown that

I tore sadly when I ran through the forest. Oh, if only I could have one new dress!"

And that evening she plagued her grandfather to give her the money to buy one.

"No! No! No!" said the woodcutter. "Your old gown is good enough for the present. If I give you one now, when the colder weather comes you will say it is not warm enough and ask for another one. When the berries turn brown, you may ask me again, and perhaps I will give you one then."

But his granddaughter could not wait till the berries turned brown.

She sulked and scolded and complained until the cottage echoed with her ill temper, and at last her grandfather gave her a silver coin to keep her quiet.

"If you cannot buy yourself a gown with

that you will have to wait till the berries turn brown," he said. "For I have no more to spare."

His granddaughter was delighted, and gave the woodcutter several kisses.

Now there was nothing to do but wait for the pedlar-woman to pass by with her silks and satins and laces, stuff for fine dresses and cloaks and petticoats.

"Stay by the door, Gobbolino!" the woodcutter's granddaughter told him as she polished the floor and wiped the dishes. "Watch for the pedlar-woman, and don't fail to tell me if you see her coming!"

Gobbolino waited many days in vain, but at last he saw the pedlar-woman approaching through the forest, with her bundles of silks, satins, and laces, all tied on the back of a little donkey that trotted beside her.

"Here she comes, mistress! Here she comes!" cried Gobbolino, and the next moment his mistress was at the door.

"Stop, good mistress! Stop!" she cried to the pedlar-woman. "Come in by my fire and have a bowl of milk, and show me some of your wares!"

The pedlar-woman laughed as she tied up her donkey outside the cottage door.

"No pretty girl has ever let me past her door without asking me to walk inside!" she cackled, stepping into the woodcutter's cottage with her arms full of her wares, which she laid on the kitchen table.

There was something about the pedlar-woman's cackle that made Gobbolino prick his ears and look at her more closely. Before he had stared at her more than a few moments he felt sure that the old woman was a witch. Only witches laughed like that, and had such long crooked fingers and such long crooked noses.

He quite made up his mind about it when the woodcutter's granddaughter began to turn over the silks and satins.

When she exclaimed:

"Oh! How I should love that crimson silk if it were only a little shade less purple!" The old woman just passed her hand over it, and – lo and behold! – it was exactly the shade the girl had dreamed of.

"Oh!" she cried. "How beautiful is this brocade! If only it had butterflies on it instead of birds!" And the next moment the birds were gone, while in their place fluttered gorgeous butterflies as large as life.

Gobbolino knew something of these tricks, but he did not like them, or the old pedlar-woman either.

He hid himself under the kitchen table and hoped nobody would notice him there.

At last the woodcutter's granddaughter chose a splendid material of sheer gold, so bright that it glittered in the sunlight. Once she had seen this she would look at nothing else.

"How much would it cost to make me a dress of this beautiful gold satin?" she asked.

"Oh, that would cost two silver pieces!" said the pedlar-woman.

"And I have only one!" cried the girl, bursting into tears of vexation.

"The scarlet is very pretty, or the green," said the pedlar-woman.

"I don't want any of them except the gold," said the girl. "Won't you take a little less for it, madam? Oh, do!"

"What! Do you wish me to give my wares away?" said the pedlar-woman in a huff, gathering up her stuffs.

"Oh, stop! Stop! Won't you take something in exchange?" begged the girl. "Won't you take my silver piece and one of those excellent dough cakes I have in the oven?"

"Dough cakes ruin my digestion!" whined the pedlar-woman. "I live on berries from the forest and clear spring water. Don't offer me your heavy dough cakes."

The woodcutter's granddaughter was offended, for she was an excellent cook, but she still wanted the gold satin very badly.

"Will you take my silk counterpane,

perhaps?" she offered. "I made it with my own hands."

"Ha! Ha! Ha!" croaked the pedlar-woman. "What should I want with a silk counterpane? I sleep in the ditches, side by side with my donkey. People would laugh to see us wrapped in silk embroidery. Don't offer me your counterpane!"

The woodcutter's granddaughter was hurt, for the counterpane was the finest thing she possessed, but she still wanted the gold satin very much indeed.

"Perhaps you would like our cuckoo-clock?" she said.

"Ho! Ho! Ho!" croaked the pedlar-woman. "I tell the time by the sun and the moon! It's the whimbrel and the lark who chime my hours. Don't offer me your cuckoo-clock!"

The woodcutter's granddaughter was very annoyed, for she had loved her grandfather's clock ever since she was a tiny girl, but the longer she looked at the gold satin the more she wanted it for her own.

"Well, I don't want any of the others," she said crossly, pushing them across the table to the pedlar-woman. "I shall just go without, that's all."

"Stop a moment, there is just one thing I will take in exchange!" said the old dame. "At present I have no cat. If you will give me the handsome cat that is hiding under your table, as well as your silver piece, I will let you have the gold satin for your dress."

"I dare not! I dare not!" said the wood-cutter's granddaughter. "The cat belongs to my grandfather, and he would never forgive me if I gave him away."

"Well, no matter," said the pedlar-woman, walking towards the door. "Perhaps your grandfather will give you another silver coin if you ask him prettily."

"But you will be gone by then!" wept the girl.

"Three miles on, through the forest, there is a tinker's hut," said the pedlar-woman. "There you can find me for the next three nights. Goodbye, my daughter."

But when the woodcutter came home, not all his granddaughter's tears and prayers could win another silver coin from him.

When he found out that she had let the pedlar-woman go he was very angry.

"What? You refused a red or a green gown for the sake of a gold one you could not buy?

Shame on you! What is one colour more than another? Now the pedlar-woman is gone, and you will have to wait for your dress until she comes back again."

The next day the woodcutter's granddaughter sulked all day long. She burned the cakes, left the pots dirty, and threw a frying pan at Gobbolino.

When her grandfather came home in the evening she begged him again to give her a silver coin, but he would not listen to her.

The next day she would not eat a thing from dawn till dark, but still he would have nothing to say when he came home to his tea.

The next day she spent weeping and walking up and down the floor, for it was the third day, and by evening the pedlar-woman would be gone.

She clenched her hands and stamped on the

floor, while Gobbolino trembled in a corner, for whenever she caught sight of him she exclaimed:

"Don't look at me like that! How dare you cast your dreadful blue eyes upon me when you have brought me to such misery! It is all your fault, I tell you, all your fault!"

But all of a sudden in the early evening her manner changed, and her unkindness towards Gobbolino turned to tenderness and compassion.

With her own hands she poured him out a saucer of cream and stood watching him drink it, murmuring:

"Beautiful Gobbolino! How handsome you are! What a shining coat you have, and what beautiful blue eyes! When you have finished your milk, Gobbolino, I have a piece of liver for you, and I believe in my drawer I have a little velvet bag that will make you a bed."

Gobbolino purred with gratitude, for the last three days had been very uncomfortable for him, and he had been very frightened of the girl's ill temper and the saucepans and frying pans that she flung at him.

"But how wrong I was to think her a shrew!" he said as he lapped the cream. "How wrong and how unkind! It comes of being born a witch's kitten, I suppose. I see the bad in other people that is in myself. The girl is young and her disappointment upset her. Her true nature is tender and bright, and how good she is to me!"

He could hear the woodcutter's granddaughter singing in her bedroom as she looked for her little velvet bag.

"Look at this, Gobbolino!" she cried as she ran into the kitchen. "Isn't this a handsome bed for you? And see! Here is a little piece of liver to go inside it, to give you pleasant dreams!"

"I thank you, dear mistress! It will make me a beautiful bed!" said Gobbolino gratefully. "But I see the sun is going down, and I must hurry off to meet my master, your grandfather."

"How ungrateful you are!" said the girl, with tears of vexation in her eyes. "Here I have given you my velvet bag for a bed and you won't even try it first!"

Gobbolino was ashamed of his carelessness when he saw how he had offended his young mistress.

"Well, I will just pop in and out again!" said he. "But I am quite sure there is no need to doubt the comfort of such an elegant bag, dear mistress."

But the girl still insisted that Gobbolino should try it for himself, so to please her he hopped inside at once.

The moment he had done so the deceitful girl drew the strings tightly, so that the mouth of the bag was closed, and he was a prisoner.

"Ha! Ha! Ha!" laughed the woodcutter's granddaughter, swinging the bag by the string. "Now you are in my power. You wicked, tiresome little cat that has brought me nothing but trouble! Now I can have my gold dress! I shall give you to the witch along with my silver piece, and I hope I may never see you again!"

"Oh, my goodness!" exclaimed Gobbolino, as the girl snatched up her bonnet and ran away through the forest swinging the velvet bag. "That I should come to this! Whatever will my master, your grandfather, say?"

"I shall tell him you ran away of your own accord!" replied the girl. "He will not find out the truth in a hurry, and the pedlar-woman will never let you go. You are going back to the place where you belong – Gobbolino the witch's cat!"

Large tears filled Gobbolino's eyes and splashed upon his shirt front as the bag swung to and fro.

The woodcutter's granddaughter was running very fast, for she was afraid the pedlar-woman would be gone, and then what was she to do for her gold dress? She was afraid, too, to be out after dark, and there were three miles to walk home when she had parted with Gobbolino.

"I will tell my grandfather I was searching for his cat," she said to herself as she hurried along, and at last the tinker's hut came in sight.

The old pedlar-woman was just on the point of departing. She was loading her wares on the back of the donkey standing before the door.

"Ho! Ho! Ho!" she croaked as the woodcutter's granddaughter arrived, quite out of breath with her haste. "I knew you were coming! *Psst!* I heard you put the cat in the bag! *Bang!* I heard you slam the door! *Pat-a-pat! Pat-a-pat!* I heard you running through the forest to meet me. You thought the old pedlar-woman would be gone!"

"Then you *are* a witch! I thought as much!" said the girl boldly. "Well, I have brought you a witch's cat! Don't let him escape, I beg of you, for if my grandfather once finds out what has happened he will turn me out of the house. Here is the cat, and here is my silver coin. Where is my gold dress?"

The pedlar-woman took the silver piece in one hand and the velvet bag in the other. She slipped the coin into her bodice, and hung the bag on the donkey's saddle.

Then she bundled up the gold material, and the woodcutter's granddaughter was so busy exclaiming over it and over all the other materials that it was almost dark when she turned to go home.

"Won't you come part of the way with me, mistress?" she asked the pedlar-woman.

"Indeed, my daughter, my way lies in the opposite direction," said the old woman. "I must be well on my journey by the time the moon rises."

"It is so far to go alone!" said the girl, clutching her roll of gold satin and peering among the trees.

"There is your little cat!" said the pedlar-woman with a malevolent smile. "You can take him back with you and give me back the dress."

"Oh, no! No! No!" cried the girl, running away through the trees as fast as her legs would carry her.

She ran so fast and so far she mistook her way and lost the path. Soon she was floundering waist-deep in brambles that clutched at her frock and tore great rents in the beautiful gold material that she carried.

She had no time to stop and cry about this, she was so far from home, and when she tried to find the path she fell into a swamp and nearly drowned herself. When she struggled out again the mud had stained the beautiful gold stuff black, and the woodcutter's granddaughter was soaked to the skin.

The moon rose, but shed no light into the inky forest, the stars twinkled, but hid their faces behind the dancing branches of the trees.

Small twigs reached out to scratch at her, twisted roots tripped her up, and the beautiful gold satin she had bought from the pedlar-woman had become a handful of muddy shreds.

When at last she reached the cottage door she was in a fever, and the woodcutter, who had been nearly mad with anxiety, put her straight to bed.

She was ill for many days, and when she recovered, her grandfather had burned the shreds of her dress in the fire, taking it for a bundle of rags.

So there she was with no dress and no Gobbolino and no silver piece, and nobody to be sorry for her either.

The woodcutter thought his cat had run away, and his granddaughter was wise enough not to tell him the truth of the adventure.

15
GOBBOLINO THE WITCH'S CAT

Meanwhile Gobbolino was travelling the roads
with the pedlar-woman, tied up in a velvet bag.
"After all, who am I to grumble at my fate?"

he said to himself. "A witch's cat I was born, and here I am a witch's cat again. If only I can escape from harming people, I will do my best to serve my mistress well, but make the innocent unhappy I never will."

And he was so meek and quiet that before long the pedlar-woman let him out of the velvet bag, and allowed him to trot along at her heels along the highway. She asked him about his home, his mother, and his little sister Sootica and encouraged him to perform his tricks whenever a crowd of children collected.

She taught him, too, to tell fortunes, but here Gobbolino soon got into trouble.

When a pretty young girl approached him, an old woman, or a handsome young man in love, he could not bring himself to chase away their smiles or their hopeful glances by telling them bad fortunes.

"Hope enough, and all you wish for will come true!" he whispered in their ears.

The pedlar-woman was very angry with him.

"You must tell them of sorrow first, and ill luck, and distress!" she told him. "Then they will be so cast down and dispirited they will come to me for a better fortune! Then I shall say you were wrong and tell them a little better fortune, but still your cruel words will ring in their ears, and they will come back again and again! Every time they do this I will tell them something a little better and something a little sadder, at the same time. And so our pockets will be full of silver!"

But Gobbolino had not the heart to bring sorrow to anyone, however false. At the sight of their distress his beautiful blue eyes filled with tears, and he told them: "Indeed, indeed, it is not true!" although his mistress beat him every time he did so.

And he did not like to see the pretty girls bringing their hard-earned pence to the pedlar-woman to exchange for ribbons, satins, and pieces of silk. He knew that the first time they tied up their hair with the ribbons, and met their lovers decked out in their new silk dresses, the ribbons would rot to shreds, and the dresses fall into fragments, for such was the witch's treachery.

"Don't buy! Don't buy!" he entreated them, but few would listen to him, and when she heard him at it the pedlar-woman boxed his ears.

At last their travels brought them to the foot of a high mountain range which the pedlar-woman told him would have to be crossed.

It seemed very high and dangerous to Gobbolino, but the donkey, who seldom spoke a word, assured him that there was a zig-zag path leading to the summit and down again the other side, and on the top there was a cave belonging to another witch, where they would probably spend the night.

Gobbolino looked forward rather fearfully to spending a night in another witch's cavern.

"But after all," he said to himself, "what else can I expect? Who am I to expect anything different? How ungrateful I am! – and how wicked! It comes of being born a witch's cat, I suppose. I had better spend the rest of my life being a proper one."

But nothing could make him harm people willingly, and the savage blackness of the mountains, the icy torrents, and the dark cavern filled him with dread.

Up and up they climbed, the pedlar-woman first, leading the little donkey, and Gobbolino last, on his three black paws, limping slightly on the white one that he had bruised with a stone.

"Perhaps one day we shall see the green fields and sunshine again!" he told himself. "And oh! How welcome they will be after this dreary witch-country!"

The higher they climbed the wilder the country became, and presently Gobbolino had the strange sensation that he had been here before.

He could not make it out at all.

"It comes of being born a witch's cat, I suppose," he said to himself. "Something inside me recognizes all this savagery, but oh! How dreary it is and how lonely!"

But the sensation grew stronger and stronger, till all of a sudden the mouth of an immense cavern yawned before them, at the entrance of which sat a black cat with emerald eyes, whom, in spite of her size, he recognized directly.

It was his little sister Sootica, and he was back on the Hurricane Mountains!

She knew him too, and her astonished cry of: "Gobbolino! My brother!" brought her mistress hurrying to the door of the cavern.

Gobbolino remembered her well, for she had not changed like his sister Sootica, whose sleek black coat, bright eyes, and forest of whiskers showed how much she enjoyed being a witch's cat.

Once her surprise was over she looked him

up and down, while the witches went into the cavern together.

"You have not grown so very much, brother!" she told him. "Your coat is almost tabby, your eyes are still blue, and only three of your paws are black. What are you doing tramping round with that old pedlar-woman, instead of living with a proper witch?"

Gobbolino had so much to tell her that he did not know where to begin.

He could only stand and look at her with joy shining in his beautiful blue eyes, as he purred over and over again:

"Oh, sister! How glad I am to see you! How well you look, and how happy! Oh, what good fortune to meet you again in this fashion, my dear sister Sootica!"

At that moment the witch called them

inside to have supper, and soon the two young cats were sharing a bowl of soup, ladled out of the familiar cauldron by the witch of the Hurricane Mountains.

"And how have you been getting on, my little man?" she asked Gobbolino, when the dishes were empty. "You can see for yourself what a fine cat your sister has become. She has learned nearly all that I can teach her. Show them some of your tricks, Sootica my dear!"

Sootica at once went through some of the more difficult tricks of witchcraft. She made beautiful music come out of the cauldron and flying pigs swoop about the room like dragonflies.

She turned Gobbolino a bright scarlet colour, which he did not like at all, and made his own mistress invisible. All this she did without winking an eyelid, so clever had she become.

"Now, show us what you can do, Gobbolino!" said the witch of the Hurricane Mountains.

"Oh, he cannot do anything at all!" said the pedlar-woman scornfully. "If you say he is brother to this handsome Sootica of yours you may be right, but he is no true witch's cat. He cannot even tell fortunes – any kitten could beat him at it. And as for his tricks, la! They are not worth a chicken's liver, sister!"

Gobbolino was so angry at her scorn, and so anxious to show his little sister Sootica that he was quite a fine fellow after all, that he began to tell the story of his adventures, beginning with his swim down the river, right down to his being sold by the woodcutter's granddaughter for a dress of gold satin.

"And here I am!" ended Gobbolino modestly, looking for his sister's praise, but she and the two witches were looking coldly at him.

"There is nothing in all your adventures that is worthy of a witch's cat," said the witch of the Hurricane Mountains. "If your mother, Grimalkin, knew what a poor thing she had reared, she would have drowned you at birth. Bah! Get into the corner there, and let us hear no more of your silly voice. Witch's cat indeed! You have the heart of a common kitchen mouser!"

Gobbolino sighed deeply as he wished the many homes that had rejected him had thought the same, but he crawled obediently into the corner and slept, while the two witches and his sister Sootica talked witchcraft half the night.

When Gobbolino awoke it was broad morning.

The fire beneath the cauldron was out, and the cavern was lit by the sun's warm rays that sent the spiders scuttling to their holes, and shamed the dusty cobwebs hanging in festoons across the craggy roof.

Wrapped in her cloak, the witch of the Hurricane Mountains snored in a corner. Sootica slept at her side, her green eyes tightly closed, but Gobbolino could not see the pedlar-woman anywhere.

He was wide awake so he thought he would go outside and talk to the donkey, but when he trotted outside, it was nowhere to be seen either.

He looked high and low, but there were only jagged rocks and precipices with a couple of ravens sitting on a nearby pinnacle that croaked at him and flapped their wings and croaked again.

Gobbolino trotted a short way up the path, but there was no sign of the donkey anywhere, so he trotted back again and sat on the threshold of the cavern basking in the sunshine, and waiting for the pedlar-woman to come and tell him where the donkey was.

The day went by and the pedlar-woman did not come. The witch and Gobbolino's little sister Sootica slept on too, while the sun mounted slowly, slowly over the top of the Hurricane Mountains, and began slowly, slowly to descend the other side.

Gobbolino sat in the entrance to the cavern basking in the sunshine and waiting for the donkey or the pedlar-woman to appear, but neither of them came, and presently long shadows crept up the side of the Hurricane Mountains and touched Gobbolino's toes with their cold blue fingers, so that he scuttled inside the cavern to escape the evening chill.

His little sister Sootica was just stirring in her corner, stretching her long and shining claws, blinking her green eyes and yawning widely as she said:

"Good-day, brother! I hope you slept well? No unpleasant dreams, I trust?"

"Oh, very well, thank you, sister," replied Gobbolino, glad to have company at last. "And you too, I hope? You have certainly slept very late."

"*Late?*" said Sootica, staring. "Why, it is barely sundown! My mistress and I never stir before the sun has set. Whatever should we do by daylight? Come, you can help me light the cauldron and prepare the evening meal."

Gobbolino obligingly blew sparks out of his whiskers until the fire began to smoke and the cauldron to bubble.

"You can be quite useful, I see!" said Sootica agreeably, casting some herbs into the mixture. "Now I think all is ready, and if you will call your mistress I will call mine, for we are ready to dine."

"I don't know where my mistress is gone to!" said Gobbolino. "I can't see her anywhere outside, and the donkey is not to be found either."

"What?" screamed his little sister Sootica. "Mistress! Mistress! Do you hear that? Gobbolino says his mistress is gone and the donkey too. When did you find that out, Gobbolino?"

"Why, early this morning when I awoke!" said Gobbolino, quite frightened at the angry glances of his sister and her mistress the witch, who had bounced out of her corner and was standing over him in a threatening attitude.

"Why didn't you go after her, you dunderhead?" she said in a fury.

"Why! I expected her to come back again at any moment!" said Gobbolino, wringing his paws and crying. "I waited all day long, but she never came! How could I tell she did not mean to return?"

"Blockhead! Numskull!" cried the witch. "Do you mean to say you have been sitting outside the whole day long without saying a word about it? Don't you know she meant to get rid of you? Don't you know she meant to leave you behind so that she would not be plagued with you any longer?"

"Oh, no! No! No!" sobbed Gobbolino. "Indeed I never thought of that, ma'am! I am very sorry to have been so foolish, but such a thought never entered my head!"

"Send him after her!" said Sootica.

"She will be a thousand leagues away by now," said the witch. "She may have been a poor witch, but she knew a trick or two, and she wouldn't be caught that way – not she! No – such a poor cat as this is not worth keeping. I shall throw him down the mountainside!"

"Oh, no! No! No!" sobbed Gobbolino, while his little sister Sootica, although rather more composed, pleaded:

"Pray, mistress, think again. He is my blood-brother and although I am very ashamed of him, I do not wish to see him die. Perhaps if we were to keep him a little while, mistress, you might teach him better ways, for you are very clever, and, after all, if you do not succeed, there is plenty of time to throw him down the mountain by and by."

"True enough," said the witch rather less fiercely. "Well, take your soup and let us get to work."

As Sootica shared her bowl of soup with him, Gobbolino thanked her gratefully for saving his life.

"Don't thank me!" said Sootica tartly. "Try to be a better cat, and worthy of our mother Grimalkin, for if you do not succeed, my mistress will certainly throw you down the mountainside and nothing that I can do will save you then."

"I will try, sister," said Gobbolino meekly.

After their meal the witch gave Gobbolino a bundle of spells to disentangle, so mixed and muddled, like a tangle of giant cobwebs, that he did not know where to begin or end.

"See, it goes like this – and this!" said Sootica, deftly dividing them with her paws, but Gobbolino fumbled and snatched at the spells, tearing and knotting them, until they were in as fine a muddle as before.

The witch and Sootica left him at it when they set out on their broomstick some time later.

Gobbolino toiled a little longer and then fell asleep, utterly weary, beside the tangle of spells.

His sister and the witch returned at dawn. The witch went straight to bed, but Sootica trotted to his side and woke him up.

"Brother! Brother! Wake up! Where are the spells? Don't you know my mistress will throw you down the mountainside if they are not ready by sunset?"

"I can't do it! Indeed I cannot!" sobbed Gobbolino, sitting up while the tears sprang to his beautiful blue eyes. "My goodness, what shall I do? What shall I do?"

"Don't cry, brother. I will help you this time, just for once!" said Sootica, and with a few deft twists of her paw the spells fell apart and lay in neat piles upon the cavern floor. "There, that is how it is done! Thus! – and thus! – and thus! Now you will know for another time! Goodnight, brother, and try to be a better cat, or my mistress will certainly throw you down the mountainside!"

"Yes, sister!" replied Gobbolino meekly, as he too curled up and slept again.

The next night the witch set Gobbolino to catch a hundred lizards for her in the rocks round the cavern. She wanted to make a very strong kind of spell, and in order to make it she must have a hundred lizards first.

So while she and Sootica flew away on the broomstick Gobbolino trotted out among the rocks, but although he saw thousands of lizards, green, scarlet, and blue ones, all frisking about in the moonlight, he could not catch a single one.

They knew all the tricks he had learned as a kitten, for they had not lived in witch-country for nothing.

When he turned himself into a piece of cheese they laughed at him and squealed like mice. When he changed into a fly they mocked and danced about the rocks like a thousand bluebottles. When he became invisible they held their sides and told him just exactly where he was hiding. Not one would come within a paw's length of him.

At last, tired out, Gobbolino crept into the cavern and fell asleep, and there his sister Sootica found him when she returned at sunrise with her mistress the witch, who went straight to sleep, wrapped in her cloak in the corner.

"Brother! Brother! Wake up, brother!" cried Sootica, shaking the sleeping Gobbolino with her paw. "Where are the hundred lizards my mistress wanted? Don't you know she will throw you down the mountainside if she does not have them by sundown?"

"Oh, I couldn't catch them, sister, indeed I could not!" sobbed Gobbolino, waking up in a hurry. "I tried and tried! They mocked and laughed at me, and would not come near me! I never even caught one, sister, and oh, my goodness, whatever is to become of me?"

"Don't cry, brother! I will help you, just this once!" said his sister Sootica, trotting out into the daylight with Gobbolino at her heels.

Out on the rocks she sat upright looking at the sun and admiring her shadow and very soon the lizards peeped out in their thousands to look at her.

"I can see you all," said Sootica sedately. "I came out to look at you and to catch a hundred of you, if I can, for my mistress to put in her spell."

"Oh, you can't catch us!" said the lizards, wriggling with delight. "Your stupid brother has been at it all day, and he hasn't so much as touched our tails!"

"Catch you indeed!" said Sootica with great contempt. "Why, I should not even try! For one thing, I do not expect there are fifty of you, far less a hundred, that are fine enough for what my mistress requires!"

This made the lizards very indignant.

"Fine enough?" they chattered. "Why, look at me! – and me! – and me! – and me!" and they came scuttling out of their holes to show Sootica how fine and handsome they were.

"Why, yes!" she said. "You will do – and you! – and you! – and you!" So saying she scooped up the first hundred that showed themselves in her paw, and stalked with them into the cavern.

"Why, how clever you are, sister!" said Gobbolino admiringly, trotting at Sootica's heels. "I played all the tricks I knew upon them, but they would not come near me!"

"Ah! You would never catch such lizards as these by witches' tricks," said Sootica wisely. "They live too near our cavern and are always in and out, they pick up everything. Go to bed now, brother, and try to be a better cat. Good-day to you."

On the third night the witch told Gobbolino to do nothing but stir the cauldron all night. She was brewing her great spell, and before she left the cavern she told the young cats about it.

"Far, far away from here there is a castle with a princess in it," she said. "Tomorrow she will be twenty-one. Twenty-one years ago, when she was born, her parents did not invite me to her christening. Now I am going to have my revenge. When this spell is ready I will mould it in the form of a golden dove. This I shall take her as a birthday present, dressed in my best clothes so she will think me her fairy godmother. But the moment she holds it in her hands the dove will peck her, and she will fall asleep for a hundred years. Then her parents will be sorry they did not invite me to her christening."

"Oh, how beautiful, mistress! How beautiful!" cried Sootica clapping her paws in delight, but Gobbolino's blue eyes grew round with horror and dismay.

"Unless the spell is put upon her on her twenty-first birthday, it will have no power over her," said the witch. "And in order to be ready it must boil all night. You must stir it, Gobbolino, and never stop a moment, or it will be spoiled."

"At least you cannot fail with that!" said Sootica joyfully, as she bade her brother goodbye, and set off behind her mistress on the broomstick.

But the moment they were gone Gobbolino sprang off the stool on which he had been standing to stir the cauldron, and began to pace up and down the cavern.

"Oh, my goodness, how wicked! How cruel! How wrong!" he said to himself. "Think of the parents' sorrow and distress! Think of the lovely girl doomed to a hundred years of sleep on her birthday! Oh, no! No! No! Never will I take part in such cruelty! Oh, why was I born a witch's cat? Oh, why?"

And leaving the cauldron to bubble as it chose, he curled up in a corner and fell asleep.

The witch and Sootica were early in returning.

All night long, as she flew about her errands, the witch had been uneasy and anxious about her spell.

"Suppose he stirs it too fast! Suppose he stirs too slowly? Suppose he lets the fire out? Or scalds himself and drops the ladle? I ought not to have left it, Sootica, for if that spell fails then all my hopes are lost."

"Indeed it cannot fail, dear mistress!" said Sootica. "Stupid and ignorant as my brother is, the merest kitten could stir a spell all night. I am sure you have no cause for fear!"

But the witch was not easy, and long before

the dawn she had turned the broomstick for home and was speeding back towards the Hurricane Mountains with the wind whistling through Sootica's whiskers as she clung behind her.

"*Whee-eew!*" they whistled, and people in the towns and villages below murmured – "There goes Sootica, the witch's cat!"

Once at the cavern's mouth the witch leapt off her broomstick and rushed inside. Sootica followed her, but more sedately, for she felt sure Gobbolino would not have been so foolish as to stop stirring the cauldron as he had been told to do so.

What was her horror to see the ashes grey under the cauldron, the bubbling silent, and worst of all, Gobbolino asleep in a ball in his usual corner!

"Miserable cat!" shrieked the witch, picking him up by the scruff of his neck. "What do you mean by this, you wretched creature?"

"It was so cruel!" sobbed Gobbolino. "I couldn't do it! Indeed I couldn't do it, ma'am!"

"*Cruel!* What word is 'cruel' for a witch's cat?" asked the witch, shaking him. "Don't you *want* to be cruel? Don't you want to be bad? Don't you want to be wicked? Don't you want to be ungrateful? You have the heart of a kitchen cat, the ambitions of a kitchen cat, and the looks of a kitchen cat! Henceforward you shall be a kitchen cat!"

And with one shriek of rage she hurled him into the cauldron.

16

GOBBOLINO THE KITCHEN CAT

The bubbles rose and broke about him as Gobbolino struggled in the cauldron. Had it been boiling he might have died, but he had let the fire out and it was almost cold.

At last the witch fished him out with a stick, and set him, dripping miserably, on the floor.

"Ho! Ho! Ho!" she jeered. "If only your mother could see you now! If she was ashamed of you before she would be ten times more so to look at you as you are this minute! Ho! Ho! Ho! Kitchen cat! Kitchen cat!"

"I should like to be a kitchen cat!" said Gobbolino. "I never wanted to be a witch's cat – not I! Witches are cruel and wicked and bad! They do evil and make people miserable! They come to a bad end, and nobody is sorry! They are bad! Bad! BAD!!"

"What! Haven't I silenced you yet?" shrieked the witch, making a snatch at him to hurl him down the mountainside, but Gobbolino skipped aside, and next moment Sootica had mounted the broomstick and called to him: "Jump up behind me, brother, quick!"

Gobbolino made one leap just as the witch made another grab at his tail.

Up-up-up! soared the broomstick, higher and higher, till the witch's shrieks and angry cries could no longer be heard and the grey peaks of the Hurricane Mountains were like shadows below.

Dizzy and sick with fright, Gobbolino could only close his beautiful blue eyes and cling to his sister Sootica as he thanked her over and over again for saving his life.

"Don't thank me!" said Sootica. "You are a disgrace to the family, and I never want to see your face again. But you are my blood-brother after all, and I did not want to see you hurled down the mountainside."

"But what will happen to you when you go back without me?" asked Gobbolino.

"Oh, pooh! I am far cleverer than my mistress the witch!" said Sootica scornfully. "She would never dare touch a hair of my head. Don't you worry about me, brother, but make up your mind to be a better cat in future. But there! I suppose it is of no use telling you that as things are now!"

Gobbolino was rather mystified by her words, but he had little breath left for wondering what she was talking about. It was all he could do to cling to the broomstick without falling off as they rushed through the air. It was ten thousand times worse than anything he had ever done before.

"Oh, please stop, sister! Oh, please! Please!

Please!" he begged, but Sootica paid no attention to him at all.

A little later he was terrified to hear her say:

"I am going to drop you now, brother. It is time I was returning home!"

"Oh, no! No! No! Sister! Whatever will become of me?" sobbed Gobbolino, but his sister only said:

"Don't be foolish! Do as I tell you, and when I say 'jump!' leave go!"

"Oh, no!" sobbed Gobbolino, clinging all the faster. "I shall be killed, indeed I shall!"

"Nonsense!" said his little sister Sootica. "Even kitchen cats land on their feet, you know!"

The next moment she cried: "Jump!" and gave him a little push with her paw.

For one terrible moment Gobbolino clung wildly, and then he fell, *down, down, down*!

Gobbolino did not open his eyes as he fell, for he expected to be killed at any minute. He did not see his sister Sootica flying away on her broomstick back to the Hurricane Mountains, nor the green grass and brown farmland coming up to meet him as he fell, nor the winding river making its indolent way through the valleys and fields.

He did not even know there was a river, until with a terrible splash the water closed over his head, and then he bounced to the surface again in a flurry of bubbles.

"Oh, I'm drowning! I'm drowning!" cried Gobbolino, and he began to swim for his life.

But where as a witch's kitten he had swum mile after mile as strongly as any little duck, now he found he could only struggle and splash, while the current carried him rapidly down towards the great mill-wheel waiting round the bend, beside the farmhouse.

It was lucky for Gobbolino that the children of the farm were playing on the bank just above the millrace.

"Look! Look!" they cried to one another. "Here comes a little cat swimming for its life!"

"It will get caught in the mill-wheel!" cried one of the little girls. "Quick! Quick! And get it out!"

Her brothers ran to get a stick, and fished out Gobbolino as they might have fished a plum out of one of their mother's pies.

"Oh! Oh! Oh!" they all cried. "He is exactly like our little Gobbolino that came swimming down the river just like that, oh, ever so long ago!"

"Gobbolino swam!" said the boys. "And this cat wasn't swimming!"

"Gobbolino's coat was nearly black," said the little girls. "And this one is quite tabby."

"But he has three black paws and one white!" they all exclaimed together. "And just look at his beautiful blue eyes!"

Gobbolino looked at them and purred and rubbed his wet body against their legs. Now that he was really a kitchen cat he found he could not speak their language any longer, but he did not mind, for they were all putting their arms about his neck and calling him their dear, long-lost Gobbolino.

"Can you still blow sparks out of your ears, Gobbolino? Can you still become invisible? Can you hide in father's shoe or in the baby's rattle?"

Gobbolino shook his head, but they still hugged and petted him and carried him up to the farm, where the farmer's wife threw up her hands to see him.

"Father! Father!" she exclaimed. "Just see what the children have found drowning in the millrace! It's the witch's kitten come back again!"

"Witches' kittens swim, they don't drown!" said the farmer, coming into the kitchen.

He took Gobbolino out of the children's hands and looked at him very carefully while the children crowded anxiously about his knee.

"That's no witch's kitten!" he said at last. "That's a common kitchen cat, that is!"

Gobbolino's grateful purrs almost choked him, while the children sang and shouted for joy at their father's words. Even the baby in the cradle – who was now sitting up and playing with a string of cotton reels – crowed with delight, so that the kitchen rang with gladness, and no one heard the sound of wheels outside until the door suddenly opened and in burst three boys, each a little bigger than the last, all shouting:

"We've come to spend the day! We've come to spend the day! We've come to spend the day!"

The next moment they had hurled them-selves on the top of Gobbolino, exclaiming:

"Oh! Oh! Oh! It's our dear, our darling, our sweet little long-lost Gobbolino! Oh where, oh where have you been? And why haven't you come to see us before?"

It was none other than the three little brothers, who had come to spend the day with the farm-children, as they often did for the benefit of their health.

The Lord Mayor's coach was even now rolling away from the door, while the baby, who had stayed outside to pick dandelions, was crawling over the lintel with angry cries at being the last to reach Gobbolino and hug him to death.

For the rest of that long, happy day the children and their long-lost friend played and gambolled about the farm, and when evening brought the Lord Mayor himself to collect the little brothers they knew that another morning would bring them back to their Gobbolino.

The farm-children, tired and hungry, trotted into the kitchen, where, beneath the trestle-table laden with good food, a saucer of cream awaited Gobbolino.

One by one the children went off to bed,

the cradle creaked its lullaby, and the farmer's wife washed the dishes.

"There are worse kitchens than this, Gobbolino, and worse homes than ours," said the farmer, filling his pipe. "While there's a fire on the hearth, there's a place beside it for you, and a saucer of milk and a bit of fish on Sundays. Is that true, mother?"

"That's true, father!" said the farmer's wife, and Gobbolino purred his gratitude.

When the dishes were wiped and put away, the farmer's wife sat in the rocking-chair gently pushing the cradle with her foot as she darned the stockings, and Gobbolino crept quietly into her lap and dozed there. He knew that he had found his home at last and for ever and ever. Nobody would turn him out again. The children would become boys and girls and men and women. The baby would grow up and rock its own baby to sleep in the wooden cradle. The farmer and his wife would grow old and watch their grandchildren and great-grandchildren toddle across the kitchen floor, and every one of them, from the oldest to the youngest born, would always have a friendly word and a place in his heart for Gobbolino the kitchen cat.

ABOUT THE AUTHOR

When Ursula Moray Williams was a little girl, she and her twin sister Barbara were sent to bed so early that they used to tell each other stories to pass the time before they went to sleep. After their mother had taught them to read and write, they began to make books – writing new stories and illustrating them with coloured pictures – which they gave to each other at Christmas or on their birthday. They made these "anniversary books" every year until they were teenagers. When they grew up, Ursula became a writer and Barbara a painter, and they remained close – although Ursula lived in England and her sister in Iceland.

Their parents, who were at one time both teachers, gave the girls and their younger brother the happiest of childhoods. The house where they lived was a huge old mansion lit by oil lamps, with an entrance hall paved in marble and surrounded by glass cases full of stuffed birds and animals – foxes, owls, weasels, jays and a large golden pheasant. The house was crumbling, and Ursula remembered that for their lessons with a governess "we moved from room to room as the ceilings fell on us." But it was a wonderful place to play in (there was a church organ that had no keyboard but provided a perfect hiding-place) – and in the big park outside they had a much-loved pony and cart.

In 1928, when the twins were nearly seventeen (they were born on 19 April 1911), they were sent to France for a year to live in a pastor's house in Annecy in the Alps. There they had to go to school – which they hated – but out of school they enjoyed every moment: swimming, climbing, skiing and picnicking in the beautiful countryside. Ursula describes this time as like living in a fairy tale. When they came home, both sisters enrolled at the Winchester College of Art, but, while Barbara thrived, Ursula dropped out after a year and decided to practise her writing at home. She was encouraged by her uncle, Stanley Unwin (who was the famous publisher of *The Hobbit*), and her first book, *Jean-Pierre*, a story set in the mountains of Annecy, was published in 1931 with her own illustrations. She remembers that the book cost just 2s 6d (12½ pence)!

In 1935 Ursula married Conrad Southey John (always called Peter after their marriage), the great-grandson of the poet Robert Southey. To him she dedicated her best-known story, *Adventures of the Little Wooden Horse* (1938), written when she was expecting their first child, Andrew. Three more sons followed – Hugh, Robin and Jamie. The four boys were taken out in the afternoons, allowing Ursula to concentrate on her writing for two hours a day, and it was during this time that she created *Gobbolino the Witch's Cat* (1942).

Ursula went on to write over seventy books for children. "I write compulsively," she said. "During the war years I was cooking for ten of us but I *had* to write, just as my twin sister had to paint and design." Her husband died in 1974, but she still lived in the family farmhouse on Bredon Hill in Gloucestershire where she brought up her children so happily. Ursula had many grandchildren and great-grandchildren. She died in October 2006.

URSULA MORAY WILLIAMS AND GOBBOLINO THE WITCH'S CAT

When **Ursula Moray Williams** created the wonderful Gobbolino, he was not the only one longing for security in a happy, loving home where he could stay "for ever and ever".

It was 1940, and in 106 continuous days of German air raid warnings, his author had become used to sheltering with her two young sons under the stairs of their Surrey home.

Bombings killed eighty-four workers in the aircraft factory where her husband worked and at another nearby, and while he was on duty as an ARP warden, an incendiary blast had hit their garage at home.

Gobbolino himself was to become a war casualty. For after the first edition sold out, the printing plates and Williams's own illustrations were lost in the Blitz. Only twenty years later was the book reissued – and became a worldwide bestseller.

Williams too was to face many crises, yet in her work for children, in many acts of kindness, and in determination, her life became as inspirational as those of her brave, fictional heroes like Gobbolino.

Ursula Moray Williams (1911–2006) wrote sixty-eight books for children, including classics such as *Adventures of the Little Wooden Horse*.

Colin Davison,
author of *Through the Magic Door: Ursula Moray Williams, Gobbolino and the Little Wooden Horse*
(Northumbria University Press)